TALES FROM THE RANGE

Illustration by Paula Geisler from *The Wilderness Outlook*, February 13–27, 1989

Tales from the Range

Stories from the Saddle

Cecil G. Emery

Ron Hamm, Editor

SUNSTONE
PRESS

SANTA FE

Sunstone books may be purchased for educational, business, or sales promotional use. For information please write: Special Markets Department, Sunstone Press, P.O. Box 2321, Santa Fe, New Mexico 87504-2321.

Book and cover design › R. Ahl
Body typeface ›
Printed on acid-free paper
∞

———————————————

Library of Congress Cataloging-in-Publication Data

Names: Emery, Cecil G., author. | Hamm, Ron, 1935- editor.
Title: Tales from the Range, Stories from the Saddle / by Cecil G. Emery ;
    Ron Hamm, editor.
Other titles: Wilderness Outlook (Silver City, New Mexico)
Description: Santa Fe : Sunstone Press, 2019. | A collection of previously
    printed newspaper columns in the Wilderness Outlook, by Cecil G. Emery,
    about his life as a cowboy and the men he knew on the range of
    Southwestern New Mexico. | "Illustration by Paula Geisler from The
    Wilderness Outlook, February 13-27, 1989."
Identifiers: LCCN 2019013289 | ISBN 9781632932624 (pbk. : alk. paper)
Subjects: LCSH: Cowboys--New Mexico--Anecdotes. | Cowboys--New
    Mexico--Folklore. | Cowboys' writings, American--New Mexico. | Ranch
    life--New Mexico--History--20th century. | New Mexico--Social life and
    customs--Anecdotes. | New Mexico--History--20th century--Anecdotes.
Classification: LCC F801 .E45 2019 | DDC 978.9/053--dc23
LC record available at https://lccn.loc.gov/2019013289

———————————————

WWW.SUNSTONEPRESS.COM
SUNSTONE PRESS / POST OFFICE BOX 2321 / SANTA FE, NM 87504-2321 /USA
(505) 988-4418 / ORDERS ONLY (800) 243-5644 / FAX (505) 988-1025

For Cecil Emery and Maclean Wilson: united by words.

Contents

Introduction

As the new year dawned in early 1988 and as he neared his eightieth birthday, Cecil Emery was asked to channel his considerable story-telling talents into a new *milieu,* i.e., the written word. Emery had spun yarns and told tales all his adult life, and it seemed natural to morph from the oral tradition he had long known to writing. There was a hitch, though, *and* it did not involve his story-telling ability. Rather, the editors of the *Wilderness Outlook* in Silver City, New Mexico, who had voted to take him on as columnist, found they couldn't decipher his hand writing. To accommodate them, he bought a second-hand typewriter and laboriously hunted-and-pecked his way into becoming a typist. With his ability to explore wider horizons now enhanced and expanded, Emery was able to hone his latent writing style and nascent narrative talent. That he did with great enthusiasm.

Long recognized for his ability to retain and convey detailed history of the past, Emery was now empowered to introduce his readers to tales from the range of southwestern New Mexico, including a long list of colorful characters with equally colorful *handles* whom he had encountered through decades of cowboying alongside them. Although he worked chiefly in the mines of New Mexico and Arizona to support first his wife Ruth and later sons James and Gary, he would turn to cowboying when mining did not offer steady work. It is from that endeavor that he met his subjects and from whence many of the tales in this book are drawn. Always he was a masterful story teller with a wry sense of humor who could have fun with his yarn-spinning but never at anyone's expense. Cowhands and others with whom he interacted bore unforgettable sobriquets bestowed upon them by their contemporaries; their nicknames are too fanciful for easy invention.

In these pages we meet "Cotton" Ernest Wrenner, "Eskimo" Daniels, Armand "Shack" Simmonds, "Big Boy" Ruebush, Charlie "Red Wolf" Hudson, Bud Reason, whose name the hands easily and quickly turned on its head to "Reasonable Bud," and even John Longbottom whose moniker "Old Longy" wasn't as catchy as his real name. In tracing the derivation of the names, Emery employed a straightforward narrative approach in exploring their genesis. "Eskimo" (Nolan) Daniels got his nickname because "he was really dark and because he never wore much clothes, even in the coldest weather." Likewise, Emery could draw us into the scenes he depicted with understatement. In talking of a longtime wilderness recluse who lived alone in a tumbledown shack he wrote, "The old shack had only pieces of roof, but it kept dry in spots." Most of his scenes were of the range but not all.

Emery related an anecdote that occurred on the streets of downtown Silver City. This one concerned the aforementioned "Old Longy." The story from Emery. "Johnny Longbottom and I were standing...on the street down from the courthouse one day when John was pretty drunk and the wind was blowing a pretty good gale. A young woman came across from the bank, started up the steps and stubbed her toe. The wind caught her dress and blew it over her head. I helped her up but John just stood there laughing. She told John that she had seen enough of him to know he was no gentleman. Johnny lisped a quick reply. "Yeth, ma'am, and I seen enough of you to know you was no gentleman either." Another story concerned a snuff-dipping range cook named Jack Rutland who was kneading bread dough one morning and looked up from his labors to see that he was being observed by someone who had walked up on him. Rutland asked the man if he was going to stay for the upcoming meal. Thereupon, the stranger replied that "it depended on which way the dip fell." Turns out, the visitor had been closely noting the snuff slowly accumulating at the end of Jack's mustache and waiting for gravity to do its work.

It is enlightening to explore his entry into newspapering. Emery employed his skills to chronicle life on the ranges and forests of the southwestern part of New Mexico in the form of newspaper columns called "Tales of New Mexico, Texas, and Arizona" in the now defunct *Wilderness Outlook*. Although Emery was a longtime miner, when not working in that field, he "cowboyed" on ranches around Silver City or for the Forest Service as a packer and fire lookout. This was the source of material for his writing. In this narrative we attempt to highlight a bit of what we consider some of the more notable of those although all of them merit reading and savoring. Given Emery's background of working in the extractive industry or ranching, the platform he utilized for his writing might appear a bit unlikely The field of conservation was not his *forte*.

In some ways, the *Outlook*, a free bi-weekly tabloid with a press run of 5,000, might be considered an unusual venue for Emery since the paper's orientation did not always find favor with its rural more conservative readers in its circulation area of Grant, Catron, Luna, and Hidalgo counties. Emery had lived, ranched, and mined in the region for decades, and some early issues of the paper were decidedly critical of those activities. Publishers/editors Paul and Kate Ciano had moved to Silver City from California intending to buy an existing newspaper. When those efforts failed, they launched the *Outlook* in the Spring of 1988. After negative reaction to some early decidedly liberal-leaning articles resulting in boycotts and withdrawal of advertising, the paper reinvented itself, running more columns, publicity handouts, book reviews, and the like. If any of this past history bothered Emery, he gave no hint of it. After all, he just wanted to tell stories. This he did throughout his tenure with the newspaper, generally keeping his narrative light although not always.

About two-thirds of his columns examined the lives of people he had known, admired, and worked with. Others were devoted to natural phenomenon such as cyclones and forest fires. Only one directly spoke of himself. That one explored his early life in Texas before moving to New Mexico where he had grown up attending a ten grade, one-room schoolhouse. There he acquired a high school education and by all accounts was a good student. He received no formal training in language use beyond what would have been expected in the time and circumstances. In the column discussing his formative years, Emery wrote of his early fascination with the dictionary. "At school there was a big dictionary and I sure used it a lot." He credited his mother with showing him how utilize it to learn the meaning of words. The etymology lessons stuck. From her he must have also acquired an affinity for languages because she could speak some French and German. He later picked up a little Navajo and Apache. Emery never stopped learning. Perhaps he remembered his school days when he later became a young instructor on the Mescalero Apache reservation near Ruidoso. Emery's ease with language shines through his work.

The "Forever Lost Cowboy" is a personal favorite and tells of an itinerant ranch hand named Jack who joined Emery's crew in 1937. It soon became apparent that the man's costly cowboying gear was considerably more polished than his range skills. Jack told everyone he had been in several Western states as a cowboy and had moved around a good deal. After observing the newcomer awhile Emery quickly came to believe it, adding: "I imagine mostly by request." Here follows an example of the newcomer's ineptitude. At nightfall after a hard day's work on the range Jack's fellow hands made up their bedrolls facing up on the downward sloping ground. Not Jack. He put his feet upward and his head down. Inevitably he kept sliding from his blankets all night. The column's title though derives from Jack's constant fear of getting lost. "When we got started...to work cattle he decided he had to have a bowel movement," Emery recalled. "He asked me to wait or he would be lost. Afterward, every time we got out of his sight, he would start squalling like a panther that he was lost." This led to one memorable episode wherein Jack soiled himself rather that stop and risk becoming separated from the rest of the crew. Emery found plenty to enjoy and write about. He saw humor everywhere.

Emery's ability to see the lighter side of life extended to wildlife. In the Gila Country he saw plenty of bears and enjoyed depicting their often-humorous antics. One column described a mother bear and her two cubs, one of which had a sense of adventure not yet matched by ursine experience. The cub had tried to take a shortcut and had become stranded on a ledge unable to descend. "[H]is mother had to explain to him that he was dumb, and would have to go where it wasn't so high. It took a little jawing on both sides, but mother knew best. When things got straightened out, they went on." Emery had wanted to get as close to the fun as he could. When the mother bear eventually noticed his temporary observation post, "I didn't have any trouble at all getting my horse started..." Another bear-focused column told of his brother-in-law who was awakened in the middle of a night at his wood-cutting site in the forest with a large bear standing astride him. The man fled in his underwear and spent the night fearful and alone shivering in the cold. The next morning workers from a nearby Civilian Conservation Corps camp found the frightened woodcutter and explained it was their pet bear which had gotten loose and had invaded his camp. Emery was also quite able to poke fun at himself. The day following his marriage Forest Service officials summoned him to lookout duty for three months until the fire season wound down. From his mountaintop aerie Emery spotted a fire near his bride's abode many miles below. "When his superior asked if he would like to investigate, Emery replied "Dadgum right!" Apparently, there was never any intent for him to look into the relatively minor blaze. Permission denied. The ribbing he took continued unceasingly. Eventually he returned to her "after my 90-day honeymoon by myself up on the Gila Wilderness." As one accustomed to spending a great deal of time in the outdoors, Emery was always interested in natural phenomena.

Therefore, it was no surprise that some of his columns were devoted to relatively unusual weather-related events such as meteorites and cyclones and one to a fire in the Black Range. Emery's encounter with a meteorite occurred in the fall of 1932 while working for the McMillan Cattle Company south of Silver City. "All of a sudden a big roar started! A second or two later, the whole country turned bright as day!... And then a huge explosion took place...I could see all the horses and men real plain." Emery also had firsthand experience with earthquakes. He either felt or heard eye-witness accounts of half a dozen. Once he encountered a friend on the ground greasing his wagon wheels. "Suddenly the wagon started shaking ... He [the friend] came out from under that wagon in a hurry!" Another time he was helping build a concrete house when a quake hit. Later he found the wall split eight inches at the top but barely affected at ground level. "We just put boards on both sides of the crack and tamped it full of cement. When we finished the house was a little out of plumb." Sixty years later Emery found the wall still standing. Emery also experienced the aftermath of cyclones. He was riding in a canyon one day with another man when they attempted to access a familiar trail only to discover it no longer existed. "All we saw was a swath 400 feet wide in which all the timber was just twisted and tangled." Nature's destructive force also manifested itself in the form of fires. The 1938 Iron Creek fire found him supporting the Forest Service as a mule skinner packing in supplies for the fire fighters. Officials were using chlorinated water which his animals refused to drink. Emery asserted himself insisting fire bosses had to provide spring water or he would withdraw his animals. They quickly acceded. Those accustomed to co-existing with nature quickly find they cope with whatever comes their way, including providing impromptu medical assistance.

Emery recounted one such experience in "A Little Corral Doctoring on the G.O.S. Ranch." Again, he managed to infuse his account of even a serious situation with humor. This instance concerned a lovesick forty-five-year-old bachelor cowboy who nearly lost both eyebrows in a freak accident. When Emery and others reached him, the man was writhing on the ground in pain. Emery found that when he tried to lift the man he was "just like a rag, but a lot heavier. His eyebrows were both loose except at each corner and they were hanging down below his lower lids." Since the party was a long way from professional medical assistance, the men debated the best course of action. The injured man said he had "a girl" who was a school teacher at Beaverhead and that she might not like him without eyebrows. Finally, someone asked Emery what first aid equipment he had in his saddle bag. The reply was a needle, black thread, and merthiolate, then widely-used as an antiseptic. An accounting of the procedure is graphic. After Emery straightened his patient's eyebrows he began sewing. He soon found that "a person's skin is pretty tough" causing him to use "the hand of an awl to force the needle through the skin." The column made no mention of anesthesia. About a month later the patient reported he was going to go "see that schoolmarm" he fancied, adding that "I think she will like me since my eyebrows look all right." Emery wrote he never learned the outcome of his patient's matrimonial quest.

Only once did Emery's writing for the *Outlook* not appear as a column but instead as a gentle rebuke to a reader's complaint about the "so-called cow pollution," chiefly "cow piles" sometimes found in the waters of the Gila Wilderness country where Emery had fished, hunted, and roamed for decades. In his rejoinder entitled "Response to Sacred Cows," Emery noted that the letter-writer was *not* from New Mexico but rather from one of the "lower states" (Louisiana.). That set the tone for Emery's comments. Pointing out that since the patties were only composed vegetation..."it would not poison him if he ate a little of it. I don't say it would taste good." Emery continued with educating the out-of-stater. "I have drunk some water that had a good percent of cow droppings *and it was wet*." As a longtime cowboy, Emery felt constrained to defend cattle. "The cows were put here the same as all other animals." He noted their value not only as food but also in providing soil nutrients from their droppings. Emery wrote of seeing cow patties used by some to heal wounds and to draw out thorns from human flesh. He advised that when "you can get something better you should..." Emery wrote that nearly anyone who had ever worked around cattle likely had ingested some of their leavings. "I never ate any animal dung intentionally..." he wrote, adding that if any had accidently done so he had not experienced any lasting ill effects. Although separated by a couple of years, two columns were long introspective pieces about the Gila Wilderness and those who inhabit such places.

Some five years before his death Emery wrote an unusually long piece entitled "My 80 Years of Ideas and Observations on the Wildlife and People Who Inhabit Good Old Mother Earth." Nearly two years later he followed it up with "A Little About the Gila Wilderness" accompanied by the headline "Cecil Emery Talks," a departure from his usual column style. Dated January 1992, it was his last. Emery began by noting that although he had spent much of his adulthood working in the Gila, he had never lost interest in it, adding that "It has some of the most beautiful places that anyone can imagine..." A bittersweet reminiscence follows: "I was young and strong then and I did enjoy the time." But unable to resist the pull of humor, he recalls a bit of doggerel he wrote on a dugout wall of one place he did not particularly care for: "I was here in 1932 and I was here in 1934, and I ain't going to be here any more." In the "Mother Earth" column Emery attempted to present a balanced view. He began by noting land abuse has always been with humankind, some brought about by man, some by animals, both domestic and wild. Of the former, he observed that "Some of this is done through greed and some of it through ignorance." This, Emery felt, was especially true in what he termed "new" lands, those used after it had lain fallow for centuries, occupied only by native creatures and indigenous peoples passing through looking for game with which to feed themselves. Emery did not name the "abusers," but perhaps he might have been thinking of those of which he had first-hand knowledge, i.e., the cattle industry, mining interests, and timbering concerns. Never identifying himself publicly as an environmentalist, Emery did note that "We are lucky enough to have some wilderness where there are no roads." He lamented, however, that the true back country was open to "Mostly strong, young people and people with plenty of money to afford pack outfits...I do not believe in ruining the land," he concluded. "Pollution should be curtailed as much as possible to try to keep every living thing as healthy as possible." All this permeated the thinking of those closest to him.

Emery's impact naturally was felt most keenly with his family. Younger son Gary, who also worked for the Forest Service before becoming an educator in Texas, recalls his father's "conversational style" As a boy, Gary slept on the front porch of the family's home. "Old timers would come past, and "I would listen to the tales coming from the living room" until with sleep-laden eyes, "I could no longer stay awake." Gary feels his father's legacy lies in imparting "a rich oral history" that he fears "we are losing." One man has taken steps to ensure this will not happen.

Maclean Wilson's vision of perpetuating the legacy of Cecil Emery as a story teller made this book possible. He wanted to share Emery's stories with others. He has done so through his support and encouragement of this project. Wilson recalls looking forward to reading Emery's columns in the *Outlook*. Even then, the old cowboy was staying engaged with a bit of fence mending and the like on ranches around town until an accident at age eighty sidelined him. Wilson had an even better relationship than mere reader. For some years he was a neighbor of Emery's in Silver City and often chatted with him during his daily walks. Wilson would pause enthralled to hear tales of days gone by. He recalls that the older man was a good story teller. "He could spin the yarns." Wilson feels Emery's longtime association with horses and those who rode them had shaped his life. Even though Emery had by then garnered local recognition, "He did not have a big ego. He was friendly, open, and likeable." Wilson believes Emery had "lessons to impart."

There is no better way to ensure that conviction than by reprinting these columns. I liked them all. Apologies in advance, but to share more here would be to do a disservice to the intent of this book. So, pick your favorites and dig in.

—Ron Hamm

HISTORICAL OUTLOOK

TALES OF NEW MEXICO, TEXAS AND ARIZONA
by Cecil G. Emery

This is the first in a series of historical articles about Grant County. Cecil Emery has lived in Grant County since 1930 except for brief spells in Arizona and Texas. He worked in the mines for 38 years as a drill operator. When the mines were down, he would work for the various ranches in the area. It is on these ranches that he heard all the colorful tales in his collection.

Journals From
(1937 - 1938)

Ben Endlich

Ben Endlich sort of went with the G.O.S. He lived on this ranch most of his life. The G. O.S. was originally the George O. Smith ranch out in the Lake Roberts area. It spread about 35 miles in both directions and fed about 3600 head of cattle. Ben lived in a room he had fixed up in the barn. He had a shop in there with a power saw and lived happily there for close to fifty years. He died there when he was in his 70's.

Ben and his mother had come to America after his father had gotten into trouble with the Church. A priest struck Ben for sleeping in church and his father rose up in a fury and killed the priest. Although he knew that his father had been caught, he never knew for certain what happened to him. While I was at the G.O.S, Ben went to his mother's funeral in California. Although he didn't believe that way, Ben buried his mother Catholic.

RE-ELECT

Michael J. Lewis

District Attorney

- Democrat -
- Experience -
- Ability -
- Integrity -

Paid for by the committee to Re-elect Michael J. Lewis, Mary Helen Chavez, Treasurer

Ben could make beautiful furniture. He would go up to Skates Canyon and cut some large cedars and have them sawed up for lumber. He made a lot of his furniture for Ruth and Hub Estes. He once made a beautiful combination solid oak chair and table. It only had two big brass screws; the rest was joined with round and square oak pegs. Ben made it for Eskimo Daniel's wife (Eskimo received his name because of the light clothing he always wore). They lived on what is now called the Gila River Ranch. The chair passed down through a chain of heirs and now my son, Jim, has it in his home in Fort Worth, Texas.

Hub Estes was one of the owners while I worked there. The other was Bull Adams. The prior owner was Vic Culberson.

In the early years, Ben had worked as a body guard for Vic so he knew how this land empire had grown. Ben intimated that Vic had hired Cruz Smith and himself to scare owners off potential sections of land. History bears this out because when these people were "gotten rid of" the outfit always wound up with the property. There was one rancher named Brennan, however, who would not be intimidated. He raised Clydesdales on a 70 acre ranch at the head of Salt Creek. Eventually, the growing G.O.S. ranch bought him out.

One related incident Ben recalled was the death of the Carpenter boy. Mrs. Carpenter was a widow and could not manage the land without the help of her 15-year-old son. Ben told me that he killed the Carpenter boy by shutting a gate in front of a bucking horse he was on. The horse hung his front feet in the gate and turned over on top of the boy, killing him.

Ben also told me the story of three men who were buried in a 40 foot ditch. They were part of a crew hired in the 1880's to dig a pipeline. It ran from a spring, over and through a ridge, to a tank in the mouth of Terry Canyon. The crew had gotten the line in and gotten the water to syphon through, but three men were still in there when the sides suddenly collapsed.

The ranch hands did not think it would do any good to dig them out. They were transient Mexican workers, so there was no way to contact their families. The men are still buried there. The pipeline still worked in the 1940's and may still yet.

Since he lived in the barn, Ben was often the first to see a visitor. He told me of one time when a man rode into the corral and lifted the lid up off the water tank (it was a very heavy lid) to let his horse drink. He then put his own head into the water tank and drank thirstily.

Ben slipped from behind the corner of the barn and shut the lid on the man's head. Even though his whole head had been dunked, he was able to raise up the lid and get out, but by then Ben was long gone.

The stranger proceeded to the ranch anyhow and Vic hired him as a ranch hand. He lasted for about two months until one day he told Vic he wanted his money. Vic wrote him a check but he refused it, possibly because he was one of many temporary ranch hands who were just a step ahead of the law. The stranger demanded cash but Vic said, "Take the check, or nothing!" The man promptly knocked Vic down, then told him with a gun in his hand to get the cash. Vic got it by hitting up all the hands for their cash.

Ben was watching this whole scene from the corner of the barn. The man hung around a little while, then Ben said he just disappeared. "

The next thing I knew," Ben said, "he just picked me up and carried me to the horse trough and slammed the lid on me. Then he ... on his horse and rode off in a leisurely fashion. The stranger's parti... words were, 'I'll shoot the first man that lifts that lid.'"

Ben said he damned near drowned before anyone had nerve enough to open the lid.

"That son of a gun," Ben said, "he knew all the time who was responsible for dunking him."

HISTORICAL OUTLOOK

TALES OF NEW MEXICO, TEXAS AND ARIZONA

By Cecil G. Emery

Tales from Grant and Catron County circa 1930s

A Biography of Shack (Armand) Simmonds

The author has lived in Grant County since 1931 except for brief spells in Arizona and Texas. He worked in the mines for 38 years as a drill operator. When the mines were down, he would work for the various ranches in the area. It is on these ranches that he heard all the colorful tales in his collection.

In the spring of 1931, my Uncle Monty Bussey and I ran into Shack Simmonds between the Y Ranch and Horse Springs in Catron County. He was about 70 years old at that time and he was working for a big sheep outfit, the Hubble Sheep Company, at the Y Ranch.

Down through the years I would meet Shack at one ranch or another and a few times in Silver City. When I did not see him, I would hear about him from other cowboys who had seen him.

In 1932 and 1933 the Forest Service decided that wild horses should be gathered up and shipped out to soap factories or removed in some other way from the forest lands. Big Boy Reubush, Sid George, Jim George, and another man who I believe was Dave Star from Deming were up on Prior Mesa above the Zigzag Trail country, trying to catch or gather the wild horses. They just had a greasy sack camp where they ran horses till they caught them, or set snares in the trails to catch them. Some snares were set to catch them by the neck; others were set over a log in the trail to catch whatever foot slipped into the snare.

One day Shack Simmonds came across a trail leading to this horse camp. The horse he was riding got a hind leg in a snare and of course he was so surprised that he went down with Shack. Shack got out of the trap but he and his horse were both skinned up considerably.

He went on down to the camp and found the men eating a meal. They hollered to Shack to get down and have something to eat with them. Shack let loose and said, "What son of a b---- set that snare in the trail?"

All the men acted like they were surprised; they asked what kind of a thing it was. Of course, as mad as Shack was, none of the men were about to acknowledge knowing what he was talking about. They would talk about it later, though, and get a good laugh. Shack told me he knew they were all lying about the snare. And he was sure that they *knew* that he knew. He laughed about it some four or five years later when he told me about it again.

In 1936, Shack was trying to hold a big, rank horse while another man, Charley Hudson, was shoeing him. The horse ran over Shack and broke his thigh. He never fully recovered from this accident, so he couldn't ride very well after that. From then on, he was usually left at the GOS Ranch headquarters. But he would go with us when we were working close by the ranch.

Shack still made a good hand. He never let anything get away because he never got off his horse, not even to urinate. He said that if a man got off a horse while he was holding cattle, the horse was likely to shake and make a racket and scare the cattle. And he was right.

I was riding a real gentle 1200 pound horse the first time I saw Shack in 1931. From then on, Shack would always tell me that if he had that good horse of mine and a good rope he could make a good start back in the cow business. He told me that he had had a large ranch up between Magdalena and Beaverhead, NM. He said he built it up with good horses and good ropes. He cut calves and unbranded grown cattle, then he drove them for 40 to 90 miles by himself. He would not get off his horse for two days or more at a time. He finally shipped two trainloads of steer to Kansas City, Kansas and Missouri.

One time he stayed on a big drunk and gambling spree for several weeks and wound up in Silver City with enough money to buy a house on Hudson Street. He gave it to his sweetie who ran a house of ill repute.

One day shortly afterwards, a notice came for him to come to the railroad depot and pick up his new Cadillac car. He said he never could remember buying it; but the freight was paid for, so he claimed it. He found a young blacksmith who said he believed he could figure out how to operate it and do mechanical work on it. It had solid leather seats but just a cloth top and curtains. He said they drove it up to Cottage San and the Silver City Water Shed at the foot of Bear Mountain when the brakes failed and it went off the road into a deep canyon. They walked back to town and never went back after it. By this time, Shack was broke and never again got away from working for wages.

Shack told me that he had been through Theological College and had learned how to be a hard shell Baptist preacher. He knew a lot of the Bible and could quote it to make it fit whatever his particular needs were at any time. This must have helped him win hearts, for even though he had no teeth and slobbered quite frequently, he would still call the madam on the phone at night after everyone else at the ranch was in bed.

But Shack was generous, if not moral. One day he gave me a new sweater and a good pair of taps (Tapaderos). I asked him where he got them and he said they were paid for, but if I didn't want them I shouldn't take them. I found out later that he had bought one of the sweaters at a local store and walked out wearing two of them. I never did find out where the taps came from.

He smoked Prince Albert tobacco. Each month he would buy two cans of this tobacco for 25 cents. That supply would last about ten days. After that, everybody else who smoked would start to come up short, even Hub Estes. Even plug tobacco was found missing. Shack once took me to the barn and showed me at least ten caches of different tobaccos he had hidden there for those times when he ran out.

Shack was cooking at the ranch once when a large group that included Jacklin, the head of Kennecott Copper, and some other Kennecott officials were there for the last day of hunting season.

We killed a beef for the meal. Shack could butcher, gut and skin a yearling beef on its hide in less than 20 minutes. He had made a son of a b---- stew and had a big pot of beans and a lot of coffee. Shack lost his pot rag at noon and kept looking for it. Meanwhile, people kept picking brown lumps out of their coffee. After they finished this noon meal, most of the men left.

Later that evening, the four of us who remained went to eat supper. The first man to dip into the big stew pot brought up the missing pot rag -- quite an appetizer! Then one man decided he would clean out a big pewter sugar bowl that held about two pounds of sugar but had no lid. When he cleaned it out, he found that the cat had gotten into the kitchen and used the sugar bowl for a sand box. That solved the mystery of the brown specks in the coffee and sugar. The man who cleaned the sugar bowl said the sugar bowl deal was no worse than the sugar factory that he had worked in.

Shack told me that he gave Ben Lilly a big pot of leftovers to take to his camp from the ranch house. He noticed that while Lilly was carrying it along, his old dog, Lilly, was eating out of the pot. Shack hollered to Ben and told him the hound was eating out of his food, and Ben Lilly said, "That's all right. She gets part of it anyway."

Shack Simmonds was finally sent to the Dry Creek Home for Old Folks. It was run by Mrs. Jessie Hines who received government assistance to house these aging citizens. This was where old Ben Lilly had wound up sometime before. Shack was sent there in the early 1940's and finally died there.

14

HISTORICAL OUTLOOK

TALES OF NEW MEXICO, TEXAS AND ARIZONA

By Cecil G. Emery

Tales from Grant and Catron County circa 1930s

The author has lived in Grant County since 1931 except for brief spells in Arizona and Texas. He worked in the mines for 38 years as a drill operator. When the mines were down, he would work for the various ranches in the area. It is on these ranches that he heard all the colorful tales in his collection.

Johnny Cravens

Johnny Cravens came to New Mexico from Louisana when he was a young man. He was 6'4" tall. Johnny Cravens worked for the LC Ranch (Tom Lyons) as General Manager from the 1880's up until the early 1900's.

He had a medium sized trunk that was half full of record books. I looked through several of these tally books and payroll books. One year's tally book showed 42,000 calves branded and 78,000 grown cows with their brands on them. This did not reflect the small outfits' stock. They also tallied 28,000 range horses with 15,000 new branded young horses one year.

Johnny married Florence Watson in the early 1900's; he was 20 years or more older than Florence. Florence was among the first students at the Normal College here at Silver City. She was here when the Big Flood came in 1904.

At that time, the Depot for the Railroad was on the lot where the American National Bank is now located. After the flood, the depot was relocated down at the south end of Bullard Street. There was no more narrow gauge going towards Pinos Altos. She said the water was in the second story of a building across College Avenue from the Farmers Market Building.

Johnny Cravens told me that he did not agree with Tom Lyons' policy of killing off a bunch of settlers to obtain land. He continued to oppose Lyons until he finally pulled up stakes. He moved down to Mexico and ranched near Casa Dublon, his property adjoining that of Pancho Villa's. He took 15,000 cattle and a good bunch of horses of his own down there.

John told me he chased Mangus Colorado from the Whitehill wells on the Mangas, down below Steins Pass. They found two men at Steins Pass hanging bottom side up. Their stomachs had burst from being filled with water anally.

He stayed in Casa Doublon till one year before Villa raided Columbus, New Mexico. Johnny had 35 men, all with Saddle Carbines. He said he gathered up 8,000 head of cattle and crossed the line. He had gotten about one mile across, three miles east of Columbus, just after sunup when Pancho Villa's men jumped them. They had quite a battle! His crew killed fifteen or more of Pancho's men and he only had one man wounded, and not very badly.

He went on to Carrizoso, New Mexico and east near Neighbors Tank and the lava beds. He ranched and mined there for many years.

Johnny told me that for several years Pancho Villa never bothered him or his stock. But then it started. He lost several thousand cattle and horses before he gave up and got out.

He told me of going to Joe and Dick Graham's rescue before leaving. He said that there were 35 or more dead Mexicans around Joe and Dick besides some that were killed that were Joe and Dick's friends. The boys had been penned down there behind their dead horses for two days and they had crawled out and gotten the dead men's guns and ammunition to keep going. I worked with Joe Graham and he told me the same story.

Johnny told me of trying to take the famous Hall boys into Silver City from Pine Cienega. He said he had them in a big, heavy buggy and got to the Metcalf place on the Mangas Lake. He had decided to camp as it was night, but some fellow came along and said he and his men were going to kill them. He gave the Hall boys their guns and they helped fight off the men. Johnny was sure Tom Lyons had sent these men to kill them.

The next day he got them to town. Sheriff Whitehill then turned them loose under bond to go back to Pine Cienega and Mule Creek. They were killed on the way back.

In a tape made by Frank Watson when he was 84 years old, he told of seeing the killing, or the results of it, a few minutes after they were killed. Johnny Cravens (alias Johnny Brunson) was Frank Watson's son-in-law.

Johnny took me to his mine in 1934 and tried to get me to work it. He had about 35 houses for workers and miners built on a winze. He took about eight million dollars worth of gold and silver out of it, but then it petered out. He sold his cattle and everything else to try and build it again. The government took the rest for the Missile Range.

Johnny was flat broke when he died. I believe he was 89 years old. His wife, Florence, lived in Central Heights, Arizona and Silver City until she was 94.

Florence knew a lot of the history of New Mexico, Arizona and old Mexico. She had learned that in New Mexico, close to the lava beds, there were caverns that held many secrets. The Apaches had hidden a lot of loot there from wagon trains and homes for miles around and away off. She had quite a few relics that she sold in Arizona. She sold some Indian relics and the mine for a little money to live on until she died.

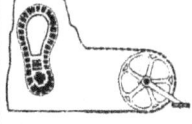

HISTORICAL OUTLOOK

TALES OF NEW MEXICO, TEXAS AND ARIZONA

By Cecil G. Emery

Tales from Grant and Catron County circa 1930s

The author has lived in Grant County since 1931 except for brief spells in Arizona and Texas. He worked in the mines for 38 years as a drill operator. When the mines were down, he would work for the various ranches in the area. It is on these ranches that he heard all the colorful tales in his collection.

ESKIMO   DANIELS

1931 - 1942

"Eskimo" (Nolan) Daniels got his nickname because he was real dark and because he never wore much clothes, even in the coldest weather. He worked out in the sticks mostly, for Heart Bar Cross, the GOS, the Hodges at XSX, and Jack Pinkerton at a hunting camp on Taylor Creek.

In the late 1920's a Russian immigrant girl came along and they got married. I used to know her given name but I have forgotten it.

Eskimo left her at the Alum Camp. Sometimes she was by herself and sometimes one of the Daniels girls stayed with her. One of Eskimo's sisters who was fourteen at the time stayed with her when her first baby girl was born. Later there was another baby girl.

When Eskimo went to work for Hub Estes, she stayed at the Goforth place on the Sapillo. After working there for awhile, he left his wife there and went to work at the hunting camp in Taylor Creek.

Ben Endlich would go see about her now and then. She had chickens, turkeys and a milk cow, and there was an old orchard for fruit.

We stacked a lot of oat hay up there and put net wire on top of the stacks so the turkeys could not scratch and ruin the hay.

When Hub and I went to the Goforth Place to see about some plowing they needed, we saw the two little girls disappear into the thickets.

We hollered and no one answered. The door was open, so we looked in and saw Eskimo's wife lying there unconscious. They had a phone so Hub got in touch with Dr. Frazen and he came out. There was a very poor road so it took awhile. He said she had a dead baby in her, which is what we had suspected.

We finally got one of the little girls to come out and she said her mother had got up on the stacks after the turkeys and fell off. Later we found out she had fallen on her belly.

Dr. Frazen cut the baby out and the woman lived. About 15 months later, she had another baby.

Charlie (Red Wolf) Hudson said not to give Eskimo's wife any groceries. I couldn't understand this since she would cook pies up and bring them to us at camp. She was always nice to us.

I told Hub what Charlie said, and Hub said to give her anything she needed that I had -- fresh meat or canned goods. Just because her husband didn't half take care of her, he said, was not any sign she and the kids should suffer.

She left the Goforth place and moved for awhile to the Threau place on the Mimbres. When she left, she did not take the solid oak chair and table combination, so later I took the chair to my house. It only had two big, brass screws in it. The rest of the chair was joined together with round and square oak pegs. It was sure heavy.

Before Eskimo left the Gila Country he was accused of branding out cattle that were mavericks. He was exonerated, but there was a stipulation -- he had to leave the vicinity. He got a job in Colorado and I lost track of them after that.

Cont'd From Page 10

all yelled for him to run. Both guns in hand, he approached Cook to make his truce.

Yes, he would surrender, but only if he could keep his weapons, travel in the back of a buckboard with his gun held on the deputy, and all accompanying cowhands must keep 30 feet away during the entire trip to the Socorro courthouse! The always fortunate Elfego even missed an ambush en route, when two separate groups of Texas avengers each mistakenly thought the other had carried out the ugly deed. He was tried twice, in both Socorro and Albuquerque, and was acquitted each time.

Everyone has heard of Tombstone Territory and Wyatt Earp. Few have heard of Gila Country or one Elfego Baca. Yet the O.K. Corral shootout involved four men against five, consumed less than a dozen rounds of ammunition, and lasted only three-fourths of a minute.

According to trial records, the "Frisco War" pitted one man against eight cowboys, lasted thirty-three hours, and burned up case after case of ammo. Witnesses spoke of counting over 4,000 holes of various calibers in the remnants of the jacal walls, with 367 in the door alone. Even the knives and forks were hit! A broom with eight holes in its handle was brought in as evidence!

Elfego Baca, Bily the Kid, Victorio, Geronimo, the taciturn grizzly bear -- each in their own way helped keep the singularly magical "wild west" WILD. The indomitable Elfego still lives, in the "wild" spirit of Gila Country.

TALES OF NEW MEXICO, TEXAS AND ARIZONA
By Cecil G. Emery

The author has lived in Grant County since 1931 except for brief spells in Arizona and Texas. He worked in the mines for 38 years as a drill operator. When the mines were down, he would work for the various ranches in the area. It is on these ranches that he heard all the colorful tales in his collection.

EARTHQUAKES IN NEW MEXICO

1928 - 1940

In 1928 there was a quake near Mountainair, New Mexico. It hit mostly in the south and left a crack across the mesa near Gran Quivira an old Indian and Spanish city now in ruins. This crack was two or three feet wide in places. It did very little damage since the few people living there were spread far apart.

Another earthquake came in the early part of 1938 while the G.O.S. outfit was camped at the mouth of the Sapillo on the Gila River. It rolled rocks off the high bluffs several times one night. Some of the boulders that came close to where the men had camped were as large as a small house! The men got up a little earlier than usual that morning. Later that year we heard of other parts of the mountain country having quakes as well.

In the early fall I came into headquarters at the G.O.S. and rode through the corrals to go down to my house. Along the way I came upon Frank Ferguson greasing his wagon. He was under a wide frame bed with a wheel slid out on the hub. Suddenly the wagon started shaking and the hogs started scattering. He came out from under that wagon in a hurry! Meanwhile my horse was stepping sideways and back and forth to accommodate the shaking ground. I rode on another quarter of a mile and just as I got to my house I felt another quake. It shook some articles off the wall in the kitchen and shook the stove pipe loose from the cook stove.

In November of 1938 I was working for the SCS (Soil Conservation Service) counting cattle. I was at Joe and Edith Hooker's ranch counting their cattle when we felt a pretty good quake one night. I had a tepee set up in the orchard close to Joe's house. Eli Clark and I were sleeping in the tepee when it shook and bumped us together in our beds.

We coud hear noise in the house and saw that everyone had gotten up. They had set up a carbide plant to light their adobe ranch house so when their chandelier broke loose and fell to the floor the gas started to escape. It had to be turned off at the carbide plant. Their china closet had fallen over so a lot of damage was done to the closet and the china inside it.

Cont'd →

→ *Cont'd*

Up Bear Creek above the ranch house were a lot of sandstone columns about 30 to 40 feet high. Many were only three or four feet wide at the bottom and about 10 to 20 feet across at the top. I though they would all be down after the quake but every one of them was still standing the next day.

Henry Woodrow (forest ranger for the Gila Wilderness for many years) told me that in 1938 he had some men working trail somewhere close to Deadman's Canyon when another quake hit that almost killed the whole crew. They were under a pretty high bluff so a lot of boulders bounced clear over all the men and horses. A few horses got skinned up. They had to quit the job they were doing and move out to some other location.

Between December, 1938 and January, 1939 I worked for Ben Avery at the K- Ranch. George Clark was there, too. We were building a concrete house just up on a point where a ridge came down to Bear Creek. We had the walls up about seven feet and we were eating supper in an old rock and adobe house that had been there for many years. We had kerosene lights but had not yet lit them so we were just sort of feeling for the things on the table.

When the quake came, Dorothy jumped about half way up and got Ben around the neck. She was hollering something, I don't remember what. When it let up shaking I started laughing and Dorothy said, "Earthquakes are not funny." My comment was that I could not see how Ben was going to help her. She then went on to explain her fears.

The barber's chair she owned had come out of a four chair barber shop in San Francisco. It was the only one to survive the quake there. She just gathered up the chair and her barbering tools and came to New Mexico. So I guess the quake brought back a lot of bad memories for her. I had my hair cut by her several times. She is still living in a rest home in Phoenix but Ben died at 94 and is buried in the Gila Mesa Cemetery.

The next day we found the wall in the new house was spread open eight inches at the top but at the ground it was barely open. We just put boards on both sides of the crack and tamped it full of cement. When we finished the house it was a little out of plumb but I think it is still standing.

Later in 1939 we felt a small quake in Bayard but I didn't hear of any damage being done. There was another small quake in the Mogollon Mountains in 1940. Since then I have not felt anything except when a plane breaks the sound barrier and causes rocks to roll off the bluffs.

I used to ride a little mule that could hear the planes coming a minute or two before I heard them. She would start getting nervous and I'd know something was going to happen. She was never wrong. It's too bad people don't have that sixth sense when it comes to earthquakes!

HISTORICAL OUTLOOK

TALES OF NEW MEXICO, TEXAS AND ARIZONA
By Cecil G. Emery

The author has lived in Grant County since 1931 except for brief spells in Arizona and Texas. He worked in the mines for 38 years as a drill operator. When the mines were down, he would work for various ranches in the area. It is on these ranches that he heard all the colorful tales in his collection.

"Cotton" Ernest Wrenner

"Cotton" Ernest Wrenner was of German descent. He was so fair-skinned that his hair and eyebrows looked like cotton which is how he got his name. He was working for George Snyder close to White Signal and the Burro Mountains in the winter of 1932.

I met him at a dance at White Signal. He did not know anyone but he never considered anyone a stranger. He found a bootlegger and bought a gallon jug and a pint bottle. He stuffed the bottle in his waistband and came in the dance hall and looked around.

There were about three young women on a bench, so he grabbed one and got on the floor and ran into everyone else instead of going with the flow of traffic. Of course, he bumped into someone and the pint bottle went down the leg of his britches and across the floor. He turned his partner loose and got on his hands and knees after the bottle. When he got it in his hand he held it way up and hollered real loud, "Everybody come on out and have a drink."

He headed for the outside and the first ones behind him were two lawmen that were there to take care of the dance. A lot more went out until the dance hall was half empty for a few minutes, or as long as it took the whole bunch to empty his bottle and the one gallon jug. They came back in and the dance went on until late. Cotton told me later that he thought that the law would get him anyway so there was no use in letting all that whiskey go to waste.

Of course, we had a woman fight, too, that night. One was red-headed. While they were down on the floor, the redhead's dress got up over her head and we could tell she was a real redhead.

A little later that year, there was a mean blizzard and Cotton rode up close to an old prospector's cabin and found a partially frozen body in an old chicken coop. He went to Taylor McDonald's house southeast of White Signal and told him. Taylor called the sheriff's office in Silver City and they told him they did not have a vehicle that would negotiate the snow drifts.

Taylor McDonald said he would bring the old man's body in on his jeep pickup. The bed was real short so the body had to be put in on an angle to fit. On the way in they skidded on the frozen ground and hit a bank to stop the truck. Taylor said Cotton told him, "You better take it easy or you'll break the old stiff's neck." When they got to the courthouse, the old man's head was rolling around loose by the body.

In the spring of 1933, Cotton came to work for the AT+ Ranch. First he built tanks at the H-L Ranch south of Silver; then when that was finished he came to ride with us. We were starting to brand new calves.

The first day he came out, the horse he was to ride had been resting for almost a month. They gave Cotton a big 1200 lb. brown horse called Dutch that acted fine most of the time when he was used regularly. When Cotton caught Dutch, I told him, "Old Dutch is sort of fresh, so you'd better watch him." He put his saddle on old Dutch and he really swelled up. Cotton slapped him on the shoulder and went on cinching up. He turned him around and led him a few feet even though the old horse was still humped up.

About thirteen of us saddled up. George Patterson caught a young horse that decided to buck. On his first jump, the flank cinch busted and then he really starting bucking. Cotton had just mounted, so he broke off to head George's horse away from a fence, but old Dutch hung his head with him and started bucking, too. When George and Cotton were thrown, they slid into neighboring fenceposts ten feet apart. Cotton's head connected with the post and he nearly busted his head open.

Cotton told me later that day that old Dutch acted so gentle that he thought I was just joking. He found out too late that I meant it.

Meanwhile I had ridden out to open a gate. Every one of the twelve horses were bucking and going all over a big flat. I think there were five loose saddles that morning.

John McMillan said, "Well, you're riding rough string and your horse was the only one that didn't buck this morning." I rode rough string about two years there and had only one horse buck. He broke his right front leg above the ankle that day and that ruined him.

A man by the name of King who was a cow buyer from Arizona told me that Cotton Wrenner was at a ranch in Southern Arizona known locally as the Strip. This camp consisted of a wire corral, a windmill and tower, and an old shack with no doors or windows left in it.

One time a horse was bucking with a young fellow on him. The horse tried to buck over a fence and fell and broke the boy's neck. It was very hot and the sheriff and doctor lived 60 miles away. All the rest left camp to go to work and Cotton stayed with the boy to wait for the sheriff.

When the sheriff arrived, Cotton was sitting in the shade of the windmill post. He asked Cotton where and how the boy was. Cotton said without getting up, "He's dead over there in the shack." King and the doctor went over there and sure enough he was there with steel traps set all the way around the body. Most of them had a housecat caught inside. These cats just multiplied in the wild at this camp. The cats were trying to eat the body.

Cotton himself told me later that the cats had started eating the boy before he even died. He couldn't keep them away so he set the traps a trapper had left on the corral fence.

A fellow from Oregon told him that if he ever came up there he would have a position for him. He got up there and he gave him a job at a big lumber company. He said, "Go over there to that office and my foreman will take care of you." Well, the foreman gave him a pick and shovel and an excavation order. "Well, he said, he learned a new word and he got the position -- the position was standing with his head and butt at the same level all day. He did not stay long, just enough to get a little eating money to come back to Arizona.

He tried to get me to go to old Mexico on a gold hunt one time but I declined. Later he came to see me from Douglas, Arizona. He said some other boys had gotten killed in Mexico trying to bring some gold out. He had married a nurse and he had his young son with him. He was crippled up with arthritis and on crutches.

Cotton always had something funny to say, even when he was badly hurt. He was a laugh for a lot of people anywhere he was. He had a lot of funny expressions and he made a lot of fun out of everything. Cotton could recite a poem and act it out. If it was sad, he cried with real tears. He changed his expression and made you see the person just as he saw that person.

He came to see me one time when he was in Silver City to see a doctor about his arthritis. We sat down to eat supper with my wife's sister and her daughters. My wife's sister, Florence Cloudt, asked after he left, "Where in the world did you run into that character?" She had got to laughing and finally had to excuse herself and go off laughing. "Is that natural?" she asked. I told her it was nothing out of the ordinary; it was very natural for him.

That visit in '58 was the last time I ever heard of Cotton.

HISTORICAL OUTLOOK

TALES OF NEW MEXICO, TEXAS AND ARIZONA

By Cecil G. Emery

The author has lived in Grant County since 1931 except for brief spells in Arizona and Texas. He worked in the mines for 38 years as a drill operator. When the mines were down, he would work for various ranches in the area. It is on these ranches that he heard all the colorul tales in his collection.

The author has lived in Grant County since 1931 except for brief spells in Arizona and Texas. He worked in the mines for 38 years as a drill operator. When the mines were down, he would work for various ranches in the area. It is on these ranches that he heard all the colorul tales in his collection.

A Little Corral Doctoring on th G.O.S. Ranch

In 1938, the G.O.S. outfit was camped at the mouth of Black Canyon and Apache Creek. There are several hot and cold springs there as well as a corral just above the campground to hold stock.

We didn't have a pasture at this camp to hold horses, so we put them against the drift fence that divides the G.O.S. and Diamond Bar Ranches. This ridge was pretty well bluffed up, so when the feed was good the horses stayed very well. The trails on the top of the ridge could be blocked to some extent by putting brush and logs across the trails; but when feed got short, the horses would hunt for a way to get out.

Everybody left to go to town except Jack Spruil and Jack Davis and me. I was instructed to work the Gila Flats and some other country before the boss came back. After working all day on the Gila Flats, we returned late in the evening. We rode off the trail back into Apache Creek which is very steep and has a lot of ledges. I was in the lead.

Suddenly Jack Davis' horse started bucking right behind me when the saddle slipped up on the horse's withers. He threw Jack over the top of me and he sailed on down the mountain into a large hole that was left when a big pine tree had been uprooted. The hole was close to four feet deep and, of course, just a nest of boulders. He hit the earth head first with his arms up by his sides. I thought the fall killed him.

(The morning after the accident on this old, gentle horse, I saw women and kids ride it. But the horse just could not stand the saddle up on his withers.)

When I got off my horse and tried to lift him, he was just like a rag, but a lot heavier. Jack Spruil got off and helped me pick him up. When we got him up and laid him flat, we saw that his head had gone through his hat which was now around his collar. His eyebrows were both loose except at each corner and they were hanging down below his lower lids.

Davis began to groan so we knew he was still alive. Jack Spruil asked for my hat and he went about 300 yards down to Apache Creek to get some water.

(Jack Spruil had cut the crown out of his own hat to let the sun try to sprout some more hair on his old bald pate. He also had a hole in the top of his head where a mule had pawed him. You could see this hole sink in when he breathed. He would pick flowers now and then and use this sinkhole as a vase for his flowers.)

When Spruil brought the hatful of water, we cleaned Davis up a little. The bleeding was light so we got him on his horse and headed for a camp about a mile up by the springs. Once there, we put him on his bed and got some hot water to clean him up a little better.

I told Davis I thought we had better try to get him to the ranch before he got too sore and stiff so he could get to a doctor.

"No," he said. "Cecil," he continued, "haven't you got a needle and thread in your war sack (just a sack with odds and ends in it). I told him I did but that I had nothing but black thread and some merthiolate (monkey blood) for medicine.

Davis told me to go ahead and sew his eyebrows back on. He said that he had a girl up at Beaverhead who was a schoolteacher and she might not like him without eyebrows.

I straightened the brows as well as I could, sterilized the needle and thread in boiling water, and started sewing. A person's skin is pretty tough. I had to use the hand of an awl to force the needle through the skin. It hurt me to force the needle through another person's skin almost as much as it hurt my patient. I've always been that way; I can feel what is hurting other people.

We got up the next morning and Davis was lucid but so sore and stiff he could hardly move at all. We went to wrangle and we found out several horses had left during the night. I sent Spruil to trail them up.

The foreman's son, Bill Hudson, an 18-year-old boy, came to camp and said Hub Estes told him to come and tell me to move camp to the mouth of the Sapillo on the Gila River that day. The boy was young and strong and willing. He also knew a little about packing and and working stock. His grandfather had raised him on a ranch near Globe, Arizona.

Bill and I packed up the camp gear and then we saddled Jack Davis' horse and put him on it. He passed out in a few minutes so we tied him in the saddle. We had the balance of the remuda and the pack outfit.

We had two choices: either go across the mountain to the camp or go down the river all the way and cross it close to a hundred times. I decided to go the mountain route.

We had not gone far up the mountain when we ran into a yellow jacket nest and really got in a wreck. We were a little past the head of Alum Canyon and had turned down around the head of Falls Canyon when the wreck took place. Three packed mules went down.

By the time night fell, we had come out on the Spring Canyon Trail to the mouth of the Sapillo. We met Hub Estes, Charlie Hudson, Claud Mattocks, and Jack Spruil with the horses that had gotten away the night before, so from there to the mouth of the Sapillo Camp we had help.

After we got to camp, we had to cook supper and put all but the night horses to pasture up on top of the hill on the Sapillo Trail. It was 11:00 p.m. by then.

The next morning, Hub told Jack Davis, "You're going out with me to a doctor." The rest of us went out to work cattle.

Hub told me that Dr. Frazen looked Davis over and let him go back to the ranch and just lay around till he got well.

"Who sewed your eyebrows back on?" Dr. Frazen asked.

"Old Cecil Emery had a needle and thread in his war sack so he sewed them back on," Davis replied.

"That's as good a job as I can do, so we won't do anything but let them finish healing," the doctor said.

Jack Davis stayed at the ranch for about a month. By then his eyebrows only showed a small scar.

"Well," Jack said as we walked into headquarters, "I'm going to Beaverhead and see that schoolmarm. I think she will still like me since my eyebrows look all right." He said he wanted to see about his homestead, too.

Davis was about 45-years-old and had never been married. I never did find out if he married the girl as that was the last I saw or heard of Jack Davis. I have often wondered if he married this girl he was so worried about.

Doc Seitzler who owned the saddle shop used to get after any of us boys that brought some patched-up jobs on our saddles or other riding equipment for him to work over. He called them "damned corral jobs." I never did many patch jobs on humans but I did a lot on horses and cattle. I was never afraid to sew up an animal or operate.

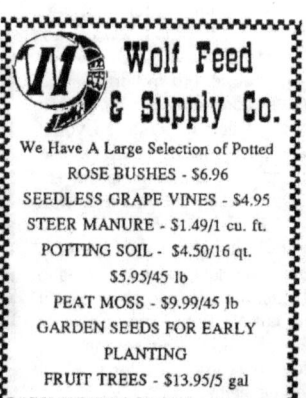

HISTORICAL OUTLOOK

GILA TRAPPERS CLUB

by Norine Thompson

Photos By Mark Erickson

When the Gila Trappers Club was formed in Silver City in 1981, Denis Murati was elected its first Booshway or president. Buckskinners elsewhere have been active for several decades.

The Gila Trappers generally wear the Western costume which prevailed during the period of 1800 to 1840 when beaver trapping dominated the North American west. Their clothing is handmade out of either leather ("buckskin"), calico, or rough homespun material which is often decorated with beadwork. Firearms, knives, tomahawks and camping equipment are also kept as authentic as possible.

The Gila Trappers (aka Mountainmen) hold a Rendezvous each March in the Gila National Forest. Buckskinners and their families from all over New Mexico, Colorado, Texas, and Arizona attend. Competitions are held in shooting, tomahawk throwing, knife throwing and lance throwing.

The most difficult competition is the Mountain Man Run in which the competitor must run a course which includes targets for pistol, rifle, tomahawk, and knife. He must also light a fire with flint and steel.

Not to be left out of the fun, women and children have their own competitions. Prizes are presented on Saturday night around the big "council fire." Most of the prizes are handmade and consist of shooting bags, knives, powder horns, beadwork, etc.

A tepee or canvas tent serves as home to the Mountainmen during the long

TALES OF NEW MEXICO, TEXAS AND ARIZONA

By Cecil G. Emery

The author has lived in Grant County since 1931 except for brief spells in Arizona and Texas. He worked in the mines for 38 years as a drill operator. When the mines were down, he would work for various ranches in the area. It is on these ranches that he heard all the colorul tales in his collection.

THE NASE ARNOLD FAMILY -- 1917 - 1935

Nase Arnold was a Norwegian from Wisconsin who came to the plains of Texas in Hale County in 1915 or 1916. He had six children. When he came, he was quite an old man. His wife seemed somewhat younger. She had one more child around 1920. Her oldest daughter had a baby girl at almost the same time.

Mr. Arnold must have had quite a bit of money, for he bought 160 acres -- one-fourth of a section of land. It was $15 - 20 an acre. They shipped about a dozen Holstein Fresian cows and some large Clydesdale horse stock which they rarely used. They just fed them. For farming purposes, they got one small Spanish mule and two burros.

They never made very good crops, and they never built very good fences. They did build a better barn than a house, although the house was somewhat better than the majority of people had in the country.

My dad, Pittman (Pit) Emery, had property on three sides of Arnold's property and the Holstein cows were regular rogues; so were the burros.

Cont'd →

weekend. Some hardy souls just wrap up in wool blankets at night.

If members feel they *must* bring modern conveniences such as motor homes or trailers, they are cast off out of sight of the "primitive" camp. Cooking is done over an open fire in cookware of the period -- mostly cast iron.

One of the pleasures of Rendezvous is to see the smoke from dozens of campfires lifting up into the tall ponderosas as people in costume move from camp to camp. Stories of the last Rendezvous are swapped as food is shared.

Becoming Mountainmen for a weekend is truly a step back in time. Members soon begin to feel that this is real life and the life they left behind is imagined.

→ Cont'd

The cows would come through the fence into our place. So my father went and fixed the fence up as the law of the country stated that each owner was to furnish half of the fence on adjoining property. All the fence so far was put up by my father. Nase told him he did not intend to furnish any fence.

The next time my father found the cows in our field he was carrying a pitchfork to handle some feed. He was on a horse, so he gave them a few prods with the fork to hurry them back to their home.

Mr. Arnold traveled 30 miles to the county seat at Plainview, Texas to swear out a warrant for molesting his livestock. So the law ordered my dad to answer at the County court house on a certain date. Eight property owners and ranchers went. They furnished the transportation as they had cars and we did not. They all went and swore that Mr. Nase Arnold's oath was not worth anything. So the judge asked Nase Arnold what he had sworn to against my father. He said that the pitchfork had inflicted a wound and the blood had run down a hill on a lakeside for about 300 feet and made a big pool of blood.

The judge threw the case against my father out and ordered Mr. Arnold to put as many wires in the fence as were needed. He also had to put a post between any existing posts belonging to other adjoining owners. They all went home.

Two days later, a deputy came down just when Mr. Arnold had set a big post about two feet from the existing corners posts and nailed two or three 2 x 4's (short) pieces so that the stock could not walk between the posts. The law had to stay and see that Mr. Arnold carried out the court orders. They had to see that every post hole was dug at least 18 inches deep. We did not have any more trouble with their cattle.

Mr. Arnold had a good-sized flint stone that he used to see clear to Planters Field in France. During World War I, he would tell us just how the battles were going.

He had the money to buy a new car, so he sent his oldest son to the Ford factory to learn how to put a new car together, how to work on it, and how to drive it back home.

When they called Benny up to go in the service, Mr. Arnold went to the draft board and told them that he had to have Benny home to take care of everything. He said that his next boy, Harmon, had his head on

crooked and was off. Harmon's head was over to one side all the time, but it did not bother him, for this happened when he was born. He was 18 years old and 6'1" tall. His bare feet measured 14 inches.

We had measured his feet at school. We used to choose sides for spelling matches and foot measurement matches on Friday evenings for entertainment.

The Arnold kids walked or rode the burros to school barefooted most of the time, even when the snow was deep. Harmon could ride real good. He wore big Chihuahua spurs and used a barbed wire for a quirt. Each one of the family had A.B.C. baking powder cans for a lunch bucket. They had the hardest baking powder biscuits and nearly always had hard boiled eggs, mostly guinea eggs. They would crack them on their foreheads. Guinea eggs are several times harder than chicken eggs.

We had a male teacher, Mr. O.C. Horn, who kept pretty good discipline. The Arnolds all had long hair. The old man said he wanted to look like Jesus Christ. Mr. Horn told the Arnold boys to get their hair cut by a certain date. All obliged him but Benny.

When recess came, Ben was told to remain. We watched from outside as Mr. Horn told Benny to sit in a chair. He did not, so Mr. Horn just picked him up and set him down so hard in a heavy oak chair that he bounced. "Now sit there!" Mr. Horn yelled, and Ben sat quietly while Mr. Horn cut his hair.

Afterwards, Mr. Horn whipped another brother, Milton, who was 16 years old (Benny was over 21). This time the Arnolds brought charges against Mr. Horn and the school board. Old man Arnold told the court that Milton wet the bed after he got the whipping. He said that the whipping had damaged Milton's kidneys. The court decided in favor of Mr. Horn.

When court got out, my father got hold of Benny. His mother told my dad to release Benny. He did, and immediately hit Benny on the chin. He flew about eight feet or more off a porch about three feet high. Before it was over, he had knocked the old man off the porch and finally slapped the old lady and the grown girl who was pummeling my father. Then Milton and Benny came after my dad, Milton with a chunk of coal and Benny with a tire iron. Both threw their weapons down and ran and it was all over that day.

For a while, Mr. Arnold dug for gold on his property. Some boys buried a pot of fool's gold in the bottom of the mine. The Arnold boys were very secretive about the mine for awhile.

Once all the kids had mumps and whooping cough. They all came to our place and skated barefoot on the ice on our water tank.

When I was 9 years old, I was hauling feed by myself one day. I had a big high load on my wagon with a spooky team. I had to go alongside of the one side of the Arnold's place that we did not own.

There were about four-to-six inch ruts in the road and I could see old man Arnold lying in one of them right in the middle of the road. The team tried to turn back. I finally hollered at him and he rose up. Finally, the team wasn't afraid anymore. I asked him why he was trying to scare my team.

Arnold explained that he was watching some little men in chariots up in the clouds running around. Then I noticed he had that flint rock up to his eye, the rock he claimed to be able to see far away with.

My father sold the property adjoining the Arnold property and I heard that they got two oil wells on their property later. Anyway, they built a good house in a town. Part of them moved there and some moved to other places like Lubbock, Texas. They still owned the original home.

Mrs. Arnold could cook real good light bread. She came to see my mother a few times. She was real nice to my mother, especially if none of her menfolk were around.

One time I was playing with a boy my age named Ray Wall. He was called "Runt" because he was short, but very active. We were about 12 years old. The two youngest Arnold boys, Leslie who was 14 and Milton who was 17, came along and started to whip us. Leslie was on Runt and Milton was on me.

Well, Runt had emptied the shot out of two or three 12 gauge shotgun shells and forced a big toad to swallow them until he couldn't hop. When Leslie started on him, Runt just picked the frog up and hit Leslie in the nose with the lead-weighted frog. That ended the fight, for Leslie's nose was very flat and very bloody. Milton was getting the worst of it, too, so they left and did not bother us for awhile.

One time someone set a stack of feed afire in the middle of the night at our place; it was a man called Leonard Harrel's feed. We kept the fire from getting to our barn or other feed we had. The stacks were full of big rats that all ran out rather than die in the fire. We had a dog that caught about a hundred rats as they were running away.

Cont'd →

→ Cont'd

We heard a car start up about a quarter of a mile away. It had a lantern for a light on the off side of the Model T Ford. It was seen again at Arnold's place by a neighbor that night.

We could never prove anything so whoever it was got away with burning the stacks. Incidentally, whoever it was, I found a French harp that was lost close to where the car was parked. If it had happened today, that probably would have been a good thing to check for fingerprints.

Just before I turned 16, I had an encounter with both of the Arnold boys, Leslie and Milton. I was by myself and I thought there were no witnesses until shortly after when I was told by an old man I knew that he had watched from behind a nearby wagon. He thought I was taking care of the problem all right so he stayed quiet.

We were having a farm implement and animal auction sale. I was changing saddles on different horses that were to be taken into the sales ring when I heard a noise. I looked around and there were Milton and Leslie Arnold. I knew by looking at Milton's face that he was all set to start something. I thought I had both of them to contend with.

Milton told me he had me dead to rights and he got in two licks to each of my eyes. I got one good one in that left his jaw teeth showing through about two inches on his left side. A few teeth had loosened so he and Leslie ran off.

I finished saddling and went into the sales ring with a horse. Both my eyes were swelling. My dad noticed it but went on with the sale (he was the auctioneer).

A friend of mine about 18 years old (Doyle Turner) saw it and asked me what happened so I told him. The sale was over with this last horse, so Doyle and I went in the direction I had seen the Arnolds going. They had entered a store. When we asked the owner, he said they had gone out the back door and were running. I knew their house and I saw them go inside it. So we just went away and thought there would be another day. I told my father what had happened. He didn't say anything except that Milton had reached 21 years of age.

The next day I didn't go to town but my dad did, and he and Milton saw each other at the same time. Papa just kept walking towards Milton and he took off running. He made it home and we heard that he left for parts unknown for quite awhile.

I saw Milton again when I was 26 years old. My brother and I were running a filling station in Lubbock, Texas. Milton Arnold came in and looked me over and said, "I've decided that fighting is not any good."

"It was only good when I was just a kid," I said. "I'm full grown now."

We did not fight anymore.

Our filling station venture did not last very long before we were broke. A gas war was on and we were independent.

I've never seen any of them since then; that was 1935.

THE EIGHT MYSTERIOUS PRINCESSES
by Natalia Avalos

Once upon a time a king and a queen had nine daughters. All of them were young and beautiful except the youngest daughter, Elizabeth. She had long hair and a couple of freckles.

One day the king and the queen were talking about the eight older daughers. The king said he would find mud on their shoes at night. But their bedroom door was locked from the outside, so how could they get out? Even the window was locked.

Without the king or the queen noticing, Elizabeth had listened to them talk. She got curious and stayed up that night but nothing happened at first.

Then she saw all her sisters except herself get up from the bed. She was amazed to see that the oldest moved one brick in the room and then a lot of bricks moved.

She followed her sisters into a very dark room. They kept on walking and walking until she saw a glow. It was outside! Then all of them started to run to the river.

When all of them got to the river they got in their boats. When they got to the end of the river, they started walking into the forest. Then they sat down, started a fire and began telling stories, playing games, and singing. The king wouldn't let them do anything except just sit in their room.

The next day Elizabeth explained everything to the king and queen. She told them they weren't letting the daughters have any fun. So the king decided to take them on a huge picnic and they all were very happy forever.

A Good Thought For Any Day
By Alma Hollis

Jesus was commanding the demon to leave him. This demon had often taken control of the man so that even when shackled with chains he simply broke them & rushed out into the desert, completely under the demon's power. - LUKE 8:29

Do you have a demon, or maybe thousands of them? Are you controlled by something in your life you don't like? Are you filled wiht despair, sadness & all tied up in knots? Well don't give up . Jesus is the answer. He can handle anything wrong in your life. Just ask & believe. Jesus can do anything

HISTORICAL OUTLOOK

TALES OF NEW MEXICO, TEXAS AND ARIZONA

By Cecil G. Emery

The author has lived in Grant County since 1931 except for brief spells in Arizona and Texas. He worked in the mines for 38 years as a drill operator. When the mines were down, he would work for various ranches in the area. It is on these ranches that he heard all the colorful tales in his collection.

JOHN LONGBOTTOM ("OLD LONGY") 1931 - 1970

Johnny Longbottom and I were standing on the corner of Bullard and the street down from the courthouse one day when John was pretty drunk and the wind was blowing a pretty good gale. A young woman came across from the bank, started up the steps, and stubbed her toe. The wind caught her dress and blew it over her head.

I helped her up but John just stood there laughing. She told John that she had seen enough of him to know he was no gentleman. Johnnny lisped a quick reply. "Yeth, ma'am, and I seen enough of you to know you was no gentleman either." He always had a ready answer, drunk or sober.

John once told me how he came to be here in the mountains. He had been working for the Diamond A Cattle Company in Engle, NM. One night he went to a community dance (he liked to dance) and got acquainted with a lot of the men but not many women, so he asked a woman to dance. She got out on the floor and she told him her name was Mary Clapp. He told her his name was John Longbottom. Mary Clapp said, "Well, Mr. Longbottom, if I had your name I would have it changed."

John replied, "You know, if I had your name, I'd go see a doctor."

Well, she turned loose and slapped hell out of John. He said everybody quit dancing and he saw Mary's dad and four brothers heading for him.

"I beat them to the door," he recounted, laughing, "and I got on my horse and just kept riding. The next day I got to the G.O.S. Ranch and went to work. I didn't ask for my pay or let anyone know where I was for a long time."

Mary Clapp was postmistress at Engle (or some post office near there) for many years, so it's probably best he kept a low profile.

Johnny had an old horse named Old Sunday. One day he got to running races with Bill Ogas for two days for a pint of whiskey per race. He and Bill would consume the pint, then he would bet again. Since John was drunk, he was not even feeding or watering poor Old Sunday, so he eventually had to pay for all the liquor. He finally went broke and I convinced him to sleep it off.

Pete Beasly told me about an incident while he and John Longbottom were working for Julian Bassett at the Heart Bars Cross up on the West fork of the Gila.

Pete and John came in one March evening and ate their dinner which consisted mostly of beans. After the meal, John went down to the barn and saddled up a horse and a pack mule but no bed. He came to the house and got the 30/30 rifle up over the door.

When Pete asked him where he was going, John said, "Well, the tumble bugs have bean hulls over their wings and can't fly, so I'm going to find a beef."

He took off to Miller Springs and came back a couple of days later with a good beef he had found over where there was no snow.

John and Pete did not agree on the bill of fare, for Pete would hardly ever eat meat. He preferred to eat beans three times a day, although he didn't care whether anyone else ate meat or not.

The two worked for several years for Julian Bassett at the Heart Bar Cross. When either Pete or John went to town, he would get drunk and stay till he was broke. Bassett would make the one left at the ranch the boss till he went to town, and then the other one would be boss. It continued like this till the ranch changed hands, I was told.

When John and Mrs. Doyle got a divorce, he got 50 cows. He moved them somewhere near Duncan, Arizona. When he got close to the new destination, he and the George Brothers started to brand them with John's brand.

The men all started drinking and finally got too drunk to finish branding the last eight head before nightfall. The next morning, the eight head had disappeared. He trailed them and discovered they had gone back to their old range.

One time when I was in town for two or three days a few of us went to the Bullard Hotel that Mrs. Ward (Jim Ward's mother) was running, and registered. Another woman was filling in for her at the time. Johnny was drunk, as was often the case, and he had been in a fight so his eyes were both swollen shut.

When Mrs. Ward came in and found John Longbottom in her hotel, she hit the ceiling and said she never wanted him in her hotel. She threatened the girl with losing her job just because she let him register. Then she told me that old son of a gun nearly crippled her friend, Mrs. Doyle, with his shenanigans in bed. I talked to her for awhile and finally talked her out of firing the girl clerk.

When John sobered up a little, Carl Starett asked him who he'd had a fight with. He looked in the mirror and said he didn't know, but he did knew that whoever it was could not do it if he was sober.

Cont'd →

HISTORICAL OUTLOOK
⟶ Cont'd

Western Art

Traditional Western painting was absent from all three exhibits. However, this legitimate, local genre has not gone out of style. Those who want to see works by one of the best local Western artists should go to K-Bob's in Deming to see *very* reasonably priced works by **Gilbert Williams.** A retired Luna County rancher, Williams shows his knowledge and love of the land in his carefully rendered oils. Williams, whose family moved to Luna County in 1875, is one of the few remaining contemporary Western artists who has actually worked the land he paints. He was a cowpuncher for over half a century.

Some years ago Southwestern New Mexican art might have been characterized as "Western" art that used realistic techniques to depict local scenes and occupations. But now diversity rules. No modern Mimbres Valley school of art has evolved, or probably ever will, at least not one using a common subject and similar techniques.

Yet a common tone, mood and approach does appear to exist among the artists of the area. The commonality surfaces when one compares their works to that of their big city counterparts.

Modern urban artists using the same techniques produce works that are tense, angular, confrontational, disruptive and controversial. It is as if they are seeking the beauty of social and psychological truths, no matter how unpleasant those truths may be to the viewer.

Compared to their urban brethren, local artists are generally more relaxed, laid-back, mystically introspective, and mellow. They seek first and last only beauty, content to let truth flow from it.

If this holds true, then it is a "school" that the ancient Mimbrenos would have understood and known as their own.

Corporate Sponsor

Eight Southwestern New Mexico artists represented by the Customs House Gallery have been selected for presentation by an Arizona business. The firm will act as their agent under a cooperative agreement, said Rosemary McLain, director of the Customs House Gallery.

The business, *Executive Decor*, a division of Statuscom Corp., is located in Tempe, Arizona. According to Barbara Smead, the company's president, *Executive Decor* will service business, financial and industrial communities by providing art for executive suites, reception areas and the like. Investment counseling regarding contemporary art will also be provided, Smead said.

Area artists selected by *Executive Decor* include: **Margot Hoylen, Dorothy Tuma, Loretta Cain, Joan Ackert, Jean Schultz, Jessica Sheldon, Allen McLain** and **Winston Sturgeon.**

Allen McLain, a master at hand-crafted furniture, is also constructing cabinets and other office furniture for *Executive Decor*.

Rosemary and Allen McLain are committed to bringing regional and national attention to Southwestern contemporary art. "We are extremely pleased that we have been able to give our artists this additional exposure and market," Mrs. McLain said. "The Southwest is an ideal place to create. But to maximize the exposure of the fine work being done here, it is helpful to have works by our artists represented by those who are geographically closer to major metropolitan areas."

Carl ran into Jim Brown in front of the Howell Drug store that morning. Jim was still drunk and could not see very well so he was feeling his way down the sidewalk. This served as pretty good evidence that Jim had also taken a beating the night before.

Carl told Jim that John Longbottom said somebody had beaten him up while he was drunk, but that that somebody couldn't do it if he was sober.

A while later, John came down the sidewalk. He was pretty sober, but still half sick. Jim Brown met him and said, "John, I hear you said some son of a gun beat you up while you was drunk. Well, you're sober and I'm still drunk, so here goes."

Well, they slugged it out for a little bit, but then Jim pulled out his knife, hung it in Johnny's mouth, and cut his cheek open to his ear on one side. John had to have some stitches and Jim went to jail for a few days.

One time I knew of Longy getting turned around while working at the G.O.S. Ranch. We were working on the west side of the Gila River on the granny benches. When it got dark we set up camp at the mouth of the Sapillo.

All of us started for the river, but Longy said we were going the wrong way. Well, we went on, and after a long while we would all stop and be still so we could hear John coming along. He never did catch up. He came into camp about 15 minutes behind us but he never did say a word.

One night at headquarters he did not come in from riding in the steer holding pasture (or elk pasture as it was also known.) After it got real dark, I could see a fire going on top of one of the bluffs about two miles west of the house.

It was pretty cold but he didn't suffer much. He came in after sun-up and told us that once he had gotten on top of the bluff, he saw that the only trail at that end was covered with solid ice. He just waited till daylight when he could see well enough to rim back around about three or four miles and come out by the Carpenter place. "Well," he said in summation, "it turned out to be a nice night to stay out and watch the stars."

Later I took hand drills and powder up to this trail that froze up in winter and drilled some bad places. I also staked some logs across to help a horse to keep from slipping, but I doubt if it was too safe even after I had done the work.

There was a sort of funny/sad incident that took place at the barn when I blasted the trail on the bluff. The explosion vibrated a lot and of course it jarred all the buildings.

Old man Ben Endlich had a room fixed up to live in the barn and when he felt and heard the shot he opened his door to investigate. Suddenly, the old shepherd dog ran in, flew under Ben's bed, and wouldn't come out.

The old dog often went with me when I went to get wood at the ranch. After I blasted big, dead trees, the dog would drag all the small pieces up to the wagon. He helped again when I put an orchard of about 25 fruit trees by the ranch house and blasted the holes for them.

I would drill about five feet deep for each tree and then put a stick of dynamite or some part of another stick inside some of them. Then I hauled a pickup load or more of dirt to fill the holes for each tree. I wanted to plant the trees in good soil from the field in Gatin Park. I would light the fuses, move back, and wait for them to go off.

Cont'd ⟶

Cont'd From Page 4

The McLains plan a "bed/breakfast/ and art room" at the Customs House for guests. They continue negotiations for regional representation of gallery artists.

April 22, 1989: In Deming, the old Customs House is designated both a state and federal historic building in a Bicentennial U.S. Customs Service celebration; the new multi-million dollar Port of Entry is dedicated at the border of Columbus, NM and Palomas, Mexico. Art exhibitions are held at both the old and the new ports of entry. Local, state and national dignitaries attend the ceremonies.

May 15, 1989: The Customs House Gallery celebrates its first anniversary. Gallery hours are 1 - 4 p.m. Monday - Friday; 1- 5 p.m. Saturday; and 1 - 3 p.m. Sun.; evening hours on Friday only 6 - 8 p.m. Admission is free.

(Donna and Dallas Johnson compiled this chronology from numerous written sources and interviews with the McLains.)

YOUTHFUL OUTLOOK

THE BOY WIZARD
by Chris Garcia
Central El. - Gr. 4

One day I was strolling through the park when I met an old man. I was surprised to see that his gray beard was two feet long.

He told me that since I was so young I was able to learn all his magic. He wanted me to learn it because he was going to die soon and I had many years left to learn and practice the magic.

He taught me first how to make myself invisible. Then the magic he taught me got harder and harder. Finally I could do the hardest trick -- create illusions.

When I had mastered all the tricks, he tested me. He lifted a 500,000,000,000 ton rock and threw it at me. I stopped it in mid-air. It wasn't very hard. It was easy.

I stayed with the wizard until the day he died. That day he left me three possessions: a bag of magic dust, a magic book, and a magic ring. He also left a note saying how to use these three items.

I practiced using these items and found they were very powerful. The ring could make time stand still. The magic book would allow me to master all the hardest spells. When I threw the magic dust on something, whatever I said should happen to that thing would happen.

I faced many dangers and these three objects helped me overcome them. Many people came to me for help and I was able to help them.

Then one day a small boy came to my house. He said that his parents had been captured by a wizard who only used black magic. His name was Abado. He captured people and used them as slaves. He had many slaves. The boy wanted me to free the slaves and his parents.

I said I would and I did. I went to the land his castle was in. It was dry and resembled a desert. I thought to myself, If I'm going to get into the castle there's going to be guards. I got out my magic dust just to be safe.

When I got to the castle I saw two men dressed in black. They were very big. I threw a pinch of dust on them. I said, "Fall asleep!" and they did.

When I entered the castle there were many hallways. It was like a maze. On each side wall there were two torches and many doors. On each door there was a lion's head carved of metal and a hole.

I looked into each hole. There were people in some rooms and some were empty. I wanted to go in the rooms so I froze time with the ring.

The first room had many people in it. In the next room, a man sat alone in a huge chair, but he wasn't frozen in time. He was the wizard.

Once I realized he was the wizard, I asked, "Why didn't you freeze in time?"

He answered, "I am a wizard. I challenge you to a wizard's duel."

I accepted the challenge.

We turned into different animals first. I turned into a cobra snake and he turned into a horse. I darted my head out to poison his leg but missed. Then I thought to myself, I came here to save some slaves, not fight.

So I took out the magic book. I put a lake under the wizard and he drowned. Then I cast a spell from the book to take me to the slaves. When I got there I saw many slaves. I cast another spell from the book that took all the slaves to their houses.

When I got home, the boy who had asked me for help was asleep, so I took him home to his parents.

I went home to sleep. Nobody could rob me because my house was invisible.

When I woke up, I was still in my house but there were people all around me. They were the castle guards. The wizard was dead but the guards weren't.

So I turned them all into huge butterflies.

They started wrecking the house so I cast a spell that vanished them to the castle.

Then I went outside to have a picnic. After finding a spot to eat I saw a small person. He gave me a small bone. He said that the old man told him to give it to me.

I asked how to use it. He said that it would make all animals either bigger or smaller and make them all like me.

I tried it on a small ant and it worked!

Later I went to the zoo because a young boy told me someone had let the lions loose.

I saw one lion under a huge tree. I hit the lion's foot with the bone and he shrank to the size of a dog. I lifted him up with a floating spell and put him into a cage. He only meowed. I hit him again with the bone and he grew back to a lion.

That was the last dangerous thing I did with the bone, the book, the ring, and the magic dust.

The magic items had done many good things. They helped a boy with a broken back, they saved a house from caving in on a family, and they even saved a baby eagle from dying.

HISTORICAL OUTLOOK
→ Cont'd

I looked back one day and old Shep had hold of one of the stope worms (fuses) in his mouth. I called him, but he just kept pulling and growling. Finally, it went off. There was a chunk of clay about the size of a wheelbarrow that went up about 20 feet with Shep on it. He went straight up and came down on top of the clay. He hit the ground with a yelp, raced past me to get to Ben Endlich's room, and ran in. I thought the blast would kill him, but it didn't. He never wanted to go after wood anymore after that, though, and I couldn't blame him.

The last time I saw John, we were both in Hillcrest Hospital. When I got able, I went to his room and talked to him. He had a leg that had been broken in a long, slanting break. They had put a bolt in it but the bone hadn't knitted up. When he tried to walk, it would make a noise. All that irritation caused it to get infected.

If he was going to patch a broken wagon tongue, I asked him, wouldn't he put at least two bolts in it? I suggested that the same approach might work better on the leg bone. John said he was going to have a little talk with his doctor about mending his leg differently.

Unfortunately, John died a short time later from that infection in his leg, I was told.

HISTORICAL OUTLOOK

TALES OF NEW MEXICO, TEXAS AND ARIZONA
by Cecil G. Emery

This is the first in a series of historical articles about Grant County. Cecil Emery has lived in Grant County since 1930 except for brief spells in Arizona and Texas. He worked in the mines for 38 years as a drill operator. When the mines were down, he would work for the various ranches in the area. It is on these ranches that he heard all the colorful tales in his collection.

THE IRON CREEK FIRE IN THE BLACK RANGE- 1938

In 1938 I was working at the G.O.S. Ranch and my wife, Ruth, and my son, Jim, were living there with me.

It was then that I ordered a washing machine from Montgomery Ward but they turned me down. They said I didn't make enough money to deserve that much credit. (At the time I made $45.00 per month along with food from the chuck wagon.)

Shortly afterwards we got a call from the Forest Service. They needed pack mules and horses for a fire on top of the Black Range. The fire camp was at Iron Creek Campground. They needed us as packers to help them move to Emory Pass.

We did not have the pack mules ready. We were camped where we could use the pickup to get supplies at the Biddle Place (where Lake Roberts is now).

We took off at about 2:00 p.m. to gather the pack mules. We had 14 head, but most of them were unshod, so we had to shoe a bunch of them.

We ran out of mule shoes so we had to make do with horse shoes. We had to cut off most of them with a coldcut to fit them onto the mules. The ends on those heels were not exactly smooth!

We also had to build sideboards for flat bed forest trucks. I had finished a good loading chute at the corrals at the Carpenter Place (Net Pasture Place) close to headquarters.

The pack mules or horses had never been loaded and hauled so they were skittish. We got some of them loaded, but then one mule with one of those freshly cut shoes reared up and caught a red mare mule on the

shoulder blade. He ripped her open to the bone, clear across her ribs to her hip bone.

Naturally, she went down, so we had to unload the truck to get her out. So we were lucky to get there with 13 mules and three horses!

We got to Emory Pass Supply Camp at 1:00 a.m. There were about 20 packers, a mix of outsiders and Forest Service people, so we surrounded the supply tent. The next morning we started to load up.

A helper and I were put in charge of eight mules. We took them to the fire line north of Emory Pass. That took us till 7:00 p.m.

The next evening I brought the animals in to rest and water. But they had chemicals in the water and none of my stock would touch it even though they were real thirsty. Of course, they wouldn't eat as long as they were still thirsty.

I told the forest officials that if they couldn't get some good water I'd pull the whole bunch. They immediately emptied the chlorinated water and hauled good spring water. Finally they started to drink and then eat. The next day I found a spring to water out at and they did even better.

There were 100 pack and riding animals and about 1100 men on this fire on Iron Creek. Three days after the fire started a rain came and put it out.

My mules were used to packing free so they all had to be tailed. They were very tired and these crews did not give them much room as they went by. So if they were not controlled, the mules woud have turned back as soon as there was room to turn around.

After the fire was out they used forest pack mules to clean

Cont'd →

Iron Creek Fire...
→ Cont'd

up and pick up tools around the fire lines. The forest ranger named Ewel Naives gave me one of the cowboys from the Diamond A Ranch to help me take my 16 head back by way of Reeds Peak McKnight Cabin. Leaving there, we'd head off to the Mimbres Lake down by the Cooney place and then on down to the G. .O. S. Headquarters.

We figured out from a map that it was a 52 mile trip, so we put in a full day. It was just daylight when we left Iron Creek and dusk when we got to headquarters. We only had to unsaddle the two saddle horses; the Forest Service hauled my pack saddles back.

The Forest Service gave me $72.00 for the packing job, so I ordered a new washing machine from Montgomery Ward and paid cash for it. Ruth told me she

would not have bought from them after they would not give me credit, but I did. In fact, I thanked them for not giving me the credit. Afterwards, they sent me a notice that my credit was good for whatever I needed. I've never used it yet.

The washing machine lasted several years till we got electricity at Whiskey Creek, which is where we lived for about 35 years.

Incidentally, the mule that got her hide ripped in the loading incident got well and was packed afterward. She had some scarring so she had to be handled sort of easy, but that was all.

Many of the people working on the fire got dysentery. It turns out that the dishwashers were not thoroughly rinsing their plates so traces of the G.I. issue yellow lye soap were being ingested. Apparently it doesn't take much lye to bring on dysentery.

On our way back to the G.O. S., we found about 30 dead cattle. They had gathered near a bluff and this cut off their oxygen supply. They alll died of smoke inhalation before the fire ever reached their area.

The loading chute was used later the same year by Will Laney to load about 500 head of big steers and some other cattle from the Heart Bar Cross up on the Gila. The cattle had been held on prior Mesa for a year or more while they were gathering them.

Then, of course, the G.O.S. and Diamond Bar cattle were loaded out from the chute after that. Everyone had been driving to ship at Fierro or even to White Water because there were not enough roads to be able to haul out on. The equipment had just begun to be built not long before that. Shortly afterwards, anyone could haul out, even for short distances.

Animals...

Both of these cats loved the outdoors and seemed quite adept at handling themselves there. They were both people shy, so they would never have gone off with a stranger even they were both beautiful enough to bring a price to a cat thief.

Once again I combed the back field daily and put up reward posters along the street, all to no avail.

This time the evidence of a violent end for my pet was even more poignant. Out in the field was a startlingly large collection of discarded containers of alcoholic beverages. There were beer bottles and cans and liquor bottles. One gallon jug looked like it held homemade whiskey -- moonshine. A large bottle of vodka bore the label "Dark Eyes." I renamed it Dark Heart.

The real evidence though was a collection of 11 fresh shotgun shells for a 20 gauge Winchester. A few of them carried the telltale message "dove and quail load," but most of them were a larger size -- 2 1/2 - 1 - 8. This must be the size they use to hunt cats.

It's not difficult to recreate the scenario. After imbibing some holiday liquor, the macho boys go out to the field to prove their manhood by shooting at anything that moves.

The remaining mystery is the whereabouts of the carcass. Do they toss it into the trash? Do they skin the animal for its pelt? I had a dream that I would see the pelts of my cats adorning someone's head in the next July 4th parade.

We need to strive to re-educate the people of this county who uphold the prevalent hunting mentality that animals are discardable commodities without rights or feelings.

Hunters need to become aware that there are those of us who are more sensitized to the animal kingdom and treat the death of a pet as they would the death of a child. Even if they regard this reaction as overly sentimental, hunters need to acknowledge and respect its existence.

Is it really male bonding between father and son to teach a child such total disregard for another life form that Dad would shoot while under the influence of alcohol?

Drunkenness among hunters is all too commonplace. They shoot randomly and often don't know or care what they've hit. Many animals suffer slow, painful deaths as the bullet burns and poisons them for a week or so.

Is this the responsibility and sensitivity we want to instill in our children?

The Bayard Police Department explained that the perpetrators of such a crime would have to be caught in the act. Since the field is on city property, the pet assassin would be fined. The amount of the fine would be deterermined by the judge. What if the judge is a sympathetic hunter? Would the fine be $1.00? Would the case be dismissed because it was "only" a cat?

The police mentioned reports of four wheelers on this property. I had also heard that hired fence menders were chased off this same property by boys conducting target practice. Do hunters have eminent domain over private property in this county? If they brazenly disregard the law so close to home, what heinous crimes against animals do they commit in the forest?

If anyone is interested in forming a volunteer, non-profit group of Animal Protectors, please call 537-5779. We need to write letters to vets asking for lowered rates on neutering; we need to create a phone tree to find homes for homeless pets; we need to trap, neuter, and re-release feral animals; we need to conduct classes to teach children how to treat their animals with respect and train them with gentleness and love.

It's an amazing discovery for some people that the more love and attention an animal receives the more human it becomes.

If we learn to be more humane and caring toward our animals perhaps we'll learn to be more humane toward one another.

If anyone sees a gray, long-haired, medium sized cat within a 10 block radius of Dayhill St. or anywhere near the border of the cow field, please call the same number -- 537-5779. There is a $25 reward for his safe return.

A GOOD THOUGHT FOR ANY DAY
by Alma Hollis

If you want a happy, good life, keep control of your tongue, and guard your lips from telling lies. Turn away from evil and do good.
1st Peter 3 - 10:11

Most everyone has told a lie sometime in their life, thinking it is the easy way out. You might get by here on earth, but each person has to stand before God sometime and answer for each one.

Maybe you didn't know, but a lie is one of the main things He says not to do.

HISTORICAL OUTLOOK

TALES OF NEW MEXICO, TEXAS AND ARIZONA

By Cecil G. Emery

The author has lived in Grant County since 1931 except for brief spells in Arizona and Texas. He worked in the mines for 38 years as a drill operator. When the mines were down, he would work for the various ranches in the area. It is on these ranches that he heard all the colorful tales in his collection.

BEN KEMP: 1931 to 1950

I got acquainted with Ben Kemp, the sheriff of Catron County, at around 1:00 a.m. in December of 1931. It was snowing heavily and had been for several days. I got Ben out of bed at that hour to give me some gas and information.

I had Shorty (Oran) Lloyd with me. We were hauling three tons of hay and one ton of grain oats on a bobtail 2 1/2 ton international truck. We were on our way to the Jewett Gap Ranger Station in Apache Creek, so we had stopped to fill up at the Catron County Junction Store and Gas Station. After visiting with Ben, we went up Apache Creek, crossing it many times for about five miles. All but a two foot width of it had frozen.

When we turned up the mountain, it got worse. We hubbed a big rock on a switchback that definitely hadn't been built for that big a truck. A three foot boulder had rolled under the differential. We couldn't go over it and we couldn't roll it out, so we had to scotch the wheels and jack the truck up to let the boulder out from under it.

We had two big screw jacks, so we raised the whole thing up by jacking under the side walls of the spare tire (high pressure). I was afraid the tire wall would give way, but it held. We let the rock out and it went off the road, bouncing through the tops of trees.

We went on our way till daylight when we topped out and our radiator boiled dry. We chopped a dead pine long and started a fire to melt snow in two ten-quart buckets. Just as the buckets were full of water, the stick holding the bucket over the fire gave way. The water turned over and nearly put the fire out, so we had to start over.

We finally got to the ranger station at 10:00 a.m. and had to wake the ranger up. He and his wife and baby were asleep by the fireplace. The ranger station barn was on a little knoll about 200 feet further; the snow between the station and the barn was about ten feet deep. When we finally got to the barn, the hay and grain had to be put in the loft. They had two horses and a milk cow, yet they had less than one bale of hay left.

We got the load unloaded and ate with the ranger family at 1:00 p.m. By 3:30, we were less than a half mile back. Empty and lightweight now, we could not go back over our tracks. We finally got enough logs pried out of the frozen ground to give the truck traction.

In March of 1932 I took another load to go to the Jewett Gap Station. I had to deliver feed to the Luna Ranger Station, too. All the snow had started to melt and the mud was as deep as the snow had been. I saw Ben Kemp on all these trips.

One night Dink Chappel and I went over the mountain to Luna after 1:00 a.m. without any lights. We had to deliver feed to sawmills and take lumber back along this unpaved, ungraveled mountain road. We would go after it froze and try to get back before it thawed.

Malin Smithson and I hauled 15,000 lbs. of lumber from Stevens' sawmill to the Gila after 9:00 p.m. at night. It took seven hours on a 2 1/2 ton truck even though the distance was only 70 miles. I also hauled Holstein cattle from Lordsburg railroad pens to the ranch up by the Jewett Gap Ranger Station for a fellow from California by the name of Jones. He had a boss at the ranch by the name of Sheppard.

Ben Kemp moved to Whiskey Creek to run a store for Art Fowler in the early 1940s. He also had a job as a peace officer for Kennecott Copper. I had occasion to have a lot of talks with Ben. He was writing a book.

We were talking about Wall Lake and Taylor Creek and he told me he was raised on Taylor Creek. There was quite a settlement there in the late 1800s and on till the early 1920s. There was even a schoolhouse. Quite a lot of Mexican people lived there; the rest were out of other states.

Ben had an uncle named Graham who had no education. He could sign his name but that was it. He set himself up as judge for the vicinity. One case he tried was when a bachelor known as Old Mike was caught butchering a two year old heifer. The judge asked him what property he owned and he admitted to owning a 30/30 rifle and a nine month old gilt (sow). Ignoring the jury, he pronounced him guilty. "I do hereby fine you one 30/30 rifle," he said, " and one nine month old gilt."

Mr. Graham had two sons, Joe and Dick. I worked with Joe at the G.O.S. ranch. Dick had a ranch close to Reserve. Joe died in Fort Bayard; Dick may have died there, too. They were both World War I vets, as was Ben Kemp.

At over 50 years of age and still without glasses, Joe Graham could still trail in a lope. I saw him break a buck's neck from the top of a running horse with only one shot. He could play any string instrument and sing a lot of songs. He claimed he could talk 28 different Mexican dialects.

Joe and Dick stayed down in Mexico for several years during the Revolution. They were both dobie-walled twice; they lived because the opposition attacked at the very last minute.

One time Joe and Dick and four or five Mexicans were jumped by a large party. Only the Graham brothers survived, and they were penned down for two days. Some of the other side were still shooting when all of a sudden some new firing started. Those not killed fled the scene. Old man Johnny Cravens and some of his men rode up. Those boys were sure glad to see that old man!

John Cravens was my wife's uncle who lived in Mexico at Casa Doublon. His ranch and Pancho Villa headquarters were less than a mile apart.

Johnny Cravens told me that Joe and Dick were the only living men left. Dead horses and about 36 dead men surrounded them. They had crawled out to these dead men and gotten their guns and ammunition to use.

Ben Kemp told me most of the people at Taylor Creek and vicinity lost their land and belongings to the war finance. The other ranches bought out the rest of the land in the late 1920s.

Ben Kemp finally moved to Carlsbad and I heard he had passed away a few years ago.

HISTORICAL OUTLOOK

TALES OF NEW MEXICO, TEXAS, AND ARIZONA

by Cecil G. Emery

Cecil Emery has lived in Grant County since 1930 except for brief spells in Arizona and Texas. He worked in the mines for 38 years. He also worked on various ranches in the area when the mines were down. It is on these ranches that he experienced all the colorful tales in his collection.

Long Green Tracks at the Head of Skates Canyon

We've chosen this story as a tribute to the noble bear since his species has suffered great losses in New Mexico this year.

A severe drought in the spring and summer led many black bears to seek food in residential areas. In Albuquerque, 11 bears were captured and released, and 8 died or were killed. In southeastern New Mexico, 21 bears were killed for eating sheep. In Silver City, one bear was killed by dogs and others were killed as predators. Of course, the mother bear who was electrocuted received worldwide attention. Altogether statewide, 53 bears were trapped or tranquilized and removed and 25 bears were destroyed.

This is quite a bit more than the average 15 a year who are hunted, so bear hunting season will hopefully be canceled.

The Animal Humane Association voted against dropping dry dog food into the drought-stricken Sandias due to potential liabilities and difficulty ensuring the bears would reach the feeding sites.

The Game and Fish Department is now planning to put big horn sheep collars on the poor remaining bears to track where they roam and what they eat. They then plan to clear small forest areas (!) to spur the growth of plants bears feed on.

When Cecil saw his bear in 1938, the species was still intact and reasonably free of man's interference except for hunters and trappers. Luckily for the bear in his story, Cecil was not one of those.

In 1938 at the GOS Ranch, we were making a drive for cattle up close to the mouth of Skates Canyon where it came into Sapillo Canyon. Hub Estes was leading the drive and he told me to go up Skates Canyon for awhile and then turn up a side canyon and come out on the right hand side at some trails heading over in Hill canyon. That way I could be in the lead to head off any cattle off that the crew drove out of Skates Canyon. I rode pretty steadily so that I would be in the right place in plenty of time.

A short time after I left the rest of the crew, I spotted three bears up in a big dead pine tree. There was a big sow bear with two good-sized cubs. One of the cubs was real black and the other one was real brown. They were about 500 feet up on a steep hillside playing in a tree about 75 feet above the ground. The cubs were having a lot of fun pulling the bark off the tree and leaning over to watch it go down and hit the ground over and over again.

I climbed up as close to the tree as my horse would go and even then the horse did not want to stay around for the fun. The old bear came down and when she hit the ground she was talking to the cubs and charging me at the same time. I didn't have any trouble at all getting my horse started since it was real scared.

When the old bear turned back to scold the cubs for not minding, they didn't mind any better than a lot of human kids. I decided to go back as close as I dared and make sure I stayed clear of the big mama. She finally got the cub down and headed up the hill with a lot of grumbling.

The cubs went a little way and then one spotted a long tall pine sapling that was leaning uphill and ran up it about 60 feet. The old bear came back and started giving him "what for" and he started back down the tree.

Just about then he lost his hold with his hind legs. His mother kept scolding him but he still could not get a hold to go either down or up. The cub did a lot of whining when he looked down. Finally, he just let go and fell about 30 feet and landed on his butt. He let out a squawk and took off after the other bear.

They were heading for a ledge that tapered off to about a foot high. At a certain point, they could switch back and continue up hill. The cub that had been the most obedient before decided to take a short cut since he had gotten a little behind. When he got to the ledge, where it was 10 feet high, his mother had to explain to him that he was dumb and he would have to go to where it wasn't so high. It took a little jawing on both sides, but mother knew best. When things got straightened out, they went on.

I realized that if I stayed any longer, I would not be where I was supposed to be, so I headed out toward the head of Skates Canyon. When I topped out right opposite the trails going out through a saddle, the ground on the hillside was chalky white. The first thing I saw was some green splattered off to the side.

Just as the trail topped out, I spotted the back end of a nearly green cow disappearing down the hillside. I could hear more and more coming. I made it in front of them and I soon saw the rest of the crew coming with a few cows.

Hub asked me where the rest of the cattle were. I told him all I had seen were some long green tracks going out over the top. He told me there were several more cattle ahead of us.

I had to ride up pretty fast after wasting so much time watching the bear show so my horse was pretty winded and sweaty, but Hub didn't say anything more. I never did tell him I had been watching the bears and messed up on my job. Quite awhile later I told some of the other boys what happened that day.

There were not too many days that we did not spill some cattle someplace. A few times we would spill them after we had them held up, especially after dark.

HISTORICAL OUTLOOK

TALES OF NEW MEXICO, TEXAS, AND ARIZONA

by Cecil G. Emery

Cecil Emery has lived in Grant County since 1930 except for brief spells in Arizona and Texas. He worked in the mines for 38 years. He also worked on various ranches in the area when the mines were down. It is on these ranches that he experienced all the colorful tales in his collection.

THE CLUB BAY ON THE G.O.S. RANCH

The location of the Wilderness Celebration is right near what was once the headquarters for the G.O.S. Ranch. In honor of this, we have chosen one of Cecil's stories that happened right in that area.

I started to work for Hub Estes at the G.O.S. Ranch on November 1, 1937. Hub instructed his foreman, Charlie (Red Wolf) Hudson that I wasn't to ride any rough horses. Then Hub left and we went to work.

We moved from headquarters to the Goforth place on the Sapillo Creek, about 10 miles away. We continued, then, without any interruption, up the north side of the Sapillo Creek into Copperas Canyon country.

It was the first day of hunting season, which lasted three weeks at that time. There were several hunters in every direction. Of course, that got the cattle all upset, not only seeing people on foot but hearing some of them shooting now and then.

I spotted one man a short way from me. Another was in a thicket on the other side of me using a turkey call.

Pretty soon a shot rang out close enough for me to hear it sing as it went by. The turkey caller came running out of the thicket hollering he had been shot.

The man that shot him came down toward me and we walked over to the turkey caller. Sure enough, he had a package of cigarettes in his shirt pocket that had been shot into. He started raising cane about a man just shooting at anything without knowing what he was shooting at.

They were arguing and I was watching so the victim asked me what I thought about it.

I told them I thought they were both crazy. I told them that all the turkey sign I had seen was old; and a man that was calling turkey in a place where there was only real old sign was as crazy as the man that just shot because he thought he heard a turkey.

They finally went on hunting and I went on hunting for cattle that we were trying to work.

Two or three days later on we were still working cattle in among the deer and turkey hunters.

I was riding a horse called Club. He was branded Club from the Club Ranch on Whiskey Creek. The horse could and would and did buck anytime and make his own excuses.

Close to the heads of the canyons there were lots of big spine cactus like small trees. Club would see a cluster of cactus and he would twist and squirm till he finally got some in his tail and flank. Then he would start bucking. The rougher the country, and the thicker the brush, the more he would turn on.

Hub had recently brought two young men out, Paul Harris and Jimmie Thompson. I was up on top above both of them. Between us there were several ledges of rock, 3 to 8 foot high bluffs that looked like big stair steps.

Suddenly, Old Club got a big cactus in his flank and tail and he turned on, jumping off the side of the ridge toward Paul and Jim. Both of them just sat there with their mouths open watching.

I yelled at them to get out of the way, but they were glued to the spot. That Club just sailed over the top of Jim's horse!

That scared Jim plenty. He said later he didn't think a horse would jump over someone that way. I told Jim it was a wonder the horse didn't jump in the middle of him and kill him.

I finally got the horse stopped. I got off and used a stick to rake the cactus off.

This same horse threw Paul Harris and crippled him for life.

When Hub came along and found me fixing to ride Club, he chewed his foreman out for having me riding the rough horse after instructing him that I was to have gentle horses.

Paul told Hub he would ride the rough string. He rode the Club horse real pretty in camp the first day, but he could not ride him in a rough place. The horse threw him off over his hips and he landed on his tailbone up on the side of No Name Canyon. He didn't get up until half an hour later when I finally got to him.

I got him up and switched our horses' saddles. He made it into camp on my horse while I rode Club.

Paul stayed in camp for several days and tried to ride again, but he couldn't sit in the saddle so he quit. He was injured so badly he failed the army examination.

I saw the Club throw several men in a year's time. There were several rough horses there, but the Club and a horse called Nine Two Bar Roan were the worst. I never rode the Nine Two Bar Roan, but I rode all the rest at one time or another. I think I could have ridden the roan, but I'll never know.

There were close to 100 horses at the GOS at the time, and one horse dragged me about half off, then threw me so high the birds could have built a nest in my butt before I hit the ground. I came down head first to keep from spraining my ankle.

I was by myself in the mouth of Black Canyon so no one saw this. The horse fell and hurt one leg so he didn't run off. I got back on him and rode him in to headquarters where I had to be helped off. By the next morning I was able enough to go back to the camp on Apache Creek close to where I was thrown the day before.

This horse bucked with me several times before this incident and some after, but he never threw me again. They told me he was a gentle horse since he never bucked unless he had you in a tight place.

31

HISTORICAL OUTLOOK

TALES OF NEW MEXICO, TEXAS, AND ARIZONA
by Cecil G. Emery

Cecil Emery has lived in Grant County since 1930 except for brief spells in Arizona and Texas. He worked in the mines for 38 years. He also worked on various ranches in the area when the mines were down. It is on these ranches that he experienced all the colorful tales in his collection.

SWAPPING PARTNERS IN 1934

In September of 1932 I formed a partnership with Elmo McMillen at the A.T. Cross. I was to ride rough string, and Elmo was to give the orders and furnish the money, chuck, and horses. It was supposed to be a steady job as long as everybody was satisfied.

Elmo said he had some little ponies that had bad habits, like throwing some of the boys away. In fact, one threw thee men off just last week. Elmo said he would give me $5 extra if I rode the rough ones. I remember that one time I counted 17 head of horses in my string. We always had 8 to 10 in the remuda at any time except in winter when we rode just three head a piece. Even with all those horses, I never had a horse throw me while I was working for McMillen. Only one horse bucked me in the time that I rode there from September, 1932 till April of 1934.

The job was steady, but he let us off from about dark till 1:00 a.m. when we were at headquarters, and till about 3:00 a.m. when we were out in one of the other camps. They furnished gray and white horses for dark nights and dark-colored horses for moonlit nights. They never came in from wrangling without most of the remuda that way.

We would always be where the cows were when the old cow rose up first thing in the morning to let the calf suck. That way the cows would not have time to hide the calves and go off and leave them.

The whole time I worked there, the A.T. Cross was under John and Elmo McMillen and their foreman Albert Wilmeth. When payday came, there was always a check ready; and we got three meals a day and plenty of it. They put a big mural (feed bag) of oats on us every morning and some kind of meat and gravy. Every meal was eaten, for you worked hard enough to give you an appetite. You would also relish the short time in bed that you were furnished if you had one at all.

About the first part of April, 1934, McMillen and I dissolved our partnership and I went job-hunting in Cliff. When I left McMillen's, Dick Hays left with me; but he went to another job at Beaverhead, NM for A. Jones.

The Black Range Road was being built so I tried for it. But Bingaman was the only contact I could find to help me get a job on the road, and that wasn't enough. I was told that if I could get Denver Littlefield or Ernest Brown to back me, they might consider me for a job some time in the future. It made me bow up to think that a simple road job required political connections.

I went looking for another job and found a job with Henry Woodrow, the Forest Ranger on the Gila Wilderness at White Creek. They were having a dry season, so Henry needed fire fighters and fence builders and fish dam builders. "I need a good cook," he said, "and I know you can make the best sourdough bread I have ever eaten. So you can go to work as long as fire season lasts or the money holds out that has been allocated for this year. In other words, it was a temporary job.

"But you will still have to go see Bingaman to get it okayed," Henry said. I then told him about the confrontation I had already had in town and he gave me a note to them. I still had to take a whole day off just to go see Bingaman and that didn't set very well with me. It still doesn't set well with me today.

During this time I worked around patching fences and doing some irrigating -- whatever I could to pay my way. I asked Ruth Watson to marry me and she said yes. I wondered how the heck I was going to manage that with no money and only a temporary job!

I went up into the mountains to work for the Forest Service. I first went with Frank Hooker from Turkey Creek with about 30 pack jacks. We went to Little Creek and there I went to building fences for gateless areas.

Then Leonard Calloway quit as cook and I took the job as chief cook and bottle washer. (There were no bottles so it wasn't too bad. George Clark was the boss on the gateless fence-building job. We had Fred Turnbaugh as powder man and driller since we had to blast in solid rock for post holes and had to blast big fallen timbers off the fence lines in a lot of places. We also had Wes Fleming and Doc Cooper as workers in the camp.

We had tents for men to sleep in and a cook tent for cooking and supplies. All the men had two seven foot logs and two four foot logs as frames around a pine needle mattress inside the tents. It kept out the cold and moisture from the ground. We seemed to be always moving camp from one location to another.

On one of the moves, George Clark's pack jack fell and rolled; the fall broke the teeth on his hair clippers. From then on, the clippers pulled out hair out instead of cutting it.

On two different trips we had to go to Fort Bayard to get more pack animals and saddles and all these jacks had to be shod. Once we got 17 head at Fierro, NM that the government leased complete with pack equipment. We had a total of 107 pack jacks that year. There were a lot of bears out hunting for food that year so we would have to go in front in pairs and keep the bears run off; otherwise, the pack train would turn back, and all of them would get down or turn the packs.

I was cooking on the east fork of Mogollon Creek during an election of county officials. Tom Holland was running for county school superintendent so some of our men went out to vote since Fred Turnbaugh was a brother-in-law to Holland. When Fred went to the Gila Settlement to vote, he did not return for several days.

Fred was an old time miner so he was handling the drilling and blasting. He also took care of storing all the explosives around camp. George Clark did all the work he could do without blasting. Finally, he told me that he would not be able to do any more till Fred got back; he did not know where the powder and fuses were, and no one there knew how to use the powder.

I told George I knew where the powder and fuses were. I told him I knew a *little* about using powder, but not a great deal. I had seen Fred climb up a trail across the canyon and up a hill. I went up the trail and up

Cont'd →

→ Cont'd

over the camp was the powder cached under a huge boulder. If it had gone off it would have covered the camp up. I brought a few sticks down to camp. I went to the foot of Fred's bed and raised up one corner and there were two metal boxes of caps and a roll of fuse.

George and I prepared the big trees that had to be shot out. When the smoke cleared, George said, "Well, it broke one end off... what happened? We had to throw a rope over the end of the log and wiggle it to make it come loose. Then we had to roll it downhill with bars to clear the fence line. By the time Fred rode into camp that night, we had all the trees cleared.

Fred had gone on a bender so he looked pretty bad, but after a good night's rest he was ready to catch up on drilling post holes. He agreed to move his cache, but he continued to keep the caps under his bed and crimp the fuse caps with his teeth even though we told him it was dangerous.

Before we left that site, George sent Doc Cooper and Wes Fleming to clear out some logs from the trails. George had told them to use a saw and axes but they went ahead and got the powder and fuses.

For the first two hours, we heard the hills shaking, and then nothing. They missed the noon meal and did not show up until about 3:00 p.m. Doc told me later that he had argued with Wes about trying to use the powder. Wes had led Doc to understand that he knew what he was doing. But Doc said he just stuck the powder on top of the log and it never splintered the top of the three foot log.

Then they had to chop it and saw it out after wasting all that time and about ten sticks of dynamite. George took him off and gave him a talking to. From what Doc told me later, he got a dressing down. Doc said George did not say much to him as he had been against taking the powder and was rightfully afraid of using it without knowing how.

When they were about ready to move camp, I took off on my horse for Cliff, NM on the evening of May 11, 1934. I went to see Malin Smithson who was working on my Model A Ford. When I saw him, he said it wasn't ready to go, but he said he would take me any place I wanted to go.

Ruth Watson and I were to be married on the twelfth of May, so on the morning of the 12th he went with us to Silver City and Judge Keener married us. Malin was a witness as well as Mrs. Dick Reese. She was the one who sold us the license.

That's when I changed partners and it has lasted for over 55 years already. I figure I got the best of the deal. I don't think Ruth had any idea what she was getting into at the time but she was stubborn enough to just stay with it through thick and thin, and there sure was a lot of the thin. We had the whole sum of $8 left when we got through with the day and I had a temporary job!

On the morning of May 13, Ruth's father came and said Henry Woodrow was hunting for me all day yesterday as a fire had broken out up in the Wilderness area. That was the reason we were up there -- to be ready to go to fires.

I headed for the camp on the East Fork of Mogollon and in a few days I was transferred to Mogollon Baldy as lookout and Curley Bryant (Lawrence) was sent up as fireman. But before we went up Curley was sent word that he and his wife, Zora (Brown) Bryant, were to have their first son born. He took off for Buckhorn and made it in time to see his son

born. When he came back, he came with a big packstring and brought back a horse of mine from the Moon Ranch.

Theron Stockbridge came up with him to work. He was walking and had his bed packed on a jack. Curley was leading my spare horse. I asked him why he didn't let Theron ride the horse. He said he suggested it, but Theron said I had threatened to whip him if I ever caught him riding one of my horses again. I had, but in this case it would have been all right, for it would have helped Curley not to have to lead the horse while he was handling a pack outfit.

When we moved from Little Creek Fire cabin to the East Fork of Mogollon Creek we had to make a new trail all the way as we went. I did not have a horse so I rode one of the pack jacks; he did not handle very well, but it beat walking.

Fred Chappell went to Little Creek Fire Cabin as fireman there that year and he told me he would never go back there. He said it was too much up edgeways and he did not like rough country.

It was 90 days from the time I went back up in the mountains after getting married till I got to go back out. From Baldy I could see Cliff on the Gila River. I could even see vehicles on the road between Cliff and Buckhorn on clear days with the field glass.

Of course, Henry Woodrow liked to joke and one day I spotted a fire at the Rice farm (I found out it was a haystack later.) I gave a reading and some other lookout gave a reading, and Henry said, "Well, wouldn't *you* like to go see about the fire?"

I told him, "Dadgum right!"

"That's pretty near Cliff, isn't it?" he continued. The ribbing I took went on all night.

It didn't rain at all till late August. It didn't rain much then either, but it was enough to let Curley Bryant go home for three or four days. When he came back, they let me go. When I came back, I packed my bed and went to White Creek Ranger Station and cooked there and packed some and went to Willow Creek to help build fish dams.

Frank Moore was in a camp there as cook and he had every bluejay and squirrel eating out of his hand or setting high up on his shoulder if no one else was around. They usually took off when someone else showed up.

I went to some small fires and a few times I had to stay out a night or two. I came by Otero's sheep camp and tried to talk them out of a lamb

Cont'd →

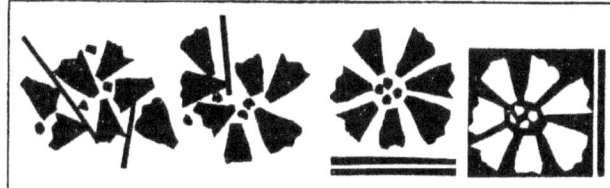

➜ Cont'd

to eat, but nothing doing. When I told Henry that story just for fun he said that a good way for a man to lose his job was to kill one of those lambs.

The Sharps had a dude camp up by White Creek called Double SS Dude Camp. Sometimes they put on quite a show for anyone coming along. They had a swimming pool and they regularly skinny-dipped, men and women. They skinny-dipped at White Creek and the main camp on Mogollon Creek as well. They would ride horses sometimes with just their shoes and swimming suits that barely covered them. How they could stand it, I don't know. They were tougher than *I* was, anyway. I would rub raw some time with all my clothes on, especially in hot weather. And the brush would keep your skin peeled up without any protection.

Sometimes some of the women and girls would come down to the Ranger Station under one pretext or another, like using a phone to call Chicago for a dinner party or date. They invariably came dressed in a halter and bikini. Henry said, "I wish I had my baby boy here so he could take care of them. His baby boy was Otho Woodrow, who was about 18 years old by then.

In August of 1934 the fire season was declared over, with 400 fires reported over the southwest forest, and I was turned loose to go home. I was told that if any money was appropriated for trail work maybe they would call us back in the fall before snow flew. But none was appropriated.

So I went home after my 90 day honeymoon by myself up on the Gila Wilderness. Ruth and I got a house from Duke Pitts on his mother's place across the Gila River from the Riverside Bridge. I got jobs bailing hay and digging potatoes and picking vegetables. I also thrashed frijole brans on the shares with a stick. Then we would catch the wind blowing and wind them out to clean them of everything but rocks.

I got a few days work on the Moon Ranch when the government was killing off a bunch of droughty cattle. They would shoot them down and guard them till they were spoiled so no one could use them for meat.

Ruth and I went to the Mimbres and got peaches and other fruit. We canned a lot of food to help us eat through that winter.

The partnership Ruth and I formed has lasted all these years and we are enjoying all our aches and pains together yet. We get together with our old friends and sometimes with new friends and compare our aches and pains and enjoy life every day.

We have two sons, Jim and Gary Emery, and five grandchildren. Jim and Mary Ellen have a girl named Diane and a son named Van. Both are in college. Gary and Linda have two sons; Scott is in high school and Chris is in junior high. They also have one daughter in grade school. All are doing well and all live in Fort Worth, Texas. JAMIE

Even though Dick Hays and I got separate jobs when we left McMillen's, we kept in touch throughout the years. Dick got married to Marie Chappel and they have done real well. They are still our close friends and neighbors.

HISTORICAL OUTLOOK

TALES OF NEW MEXICO, TEXAS, AND ARIZONA

by Cecil G. Emery

Cecil Emery has lived in Grant County since 1930 except for brief spells in Arizona and Texas. He worked in the mines for 38 years. He also worked on various ranches in the area when the mines were down. It is on these ranches that he experienced all the colorful tales in his collection.

GEORGE AND ELI CLARK IN 1931

I met George Clark for the first time in July of 1931 and Eli soon after that. George lived in Gila with his family of two small boys and one small girl and his wife and three grown stepdaughters, one single and two married.

George was a cowboy, carpenter, and farmer and he could build good log houses. He was handy about anything to be done and could get along wtih any man. He could move cattle without chousing them, and also keep the horses and men in good shape.

Geoge had another brother, Will Clark at Pleasanton, close to Glenwood, but George and Eli I knew real well.

George was foreman for the Moon Ranch under John McDermott who was the manager for Julian Basset. He and Bud Reason (we called him "Reasonable Bud") built a store and office at Gila for Bassett, as well as a two room log cabin on Prior Mesa with a double fireplace between for both rooms.

George and I worked together for the Forest Service fighting fires, building fish dams in streams, and building gateless area fences. We packed together, too.

One time we were going up the trail to White Creek and there was still deep snow in places. George's bed jack slipped and fell in the head of the canyon in several feet of snow. He had a hair-cutting outfit in his bed.

George had a habit as all the Clarks did of screwing up their faces when they were going to say anything, sort of like it hurt to talk. So George squinched and said, "There goes my clippers." Sure enough, when we got the jack out and got to camp, the clippers had about three teeth broken out. It sure would pull hair out after that, but that's the way we got our ears lowered for several months at a time.

George told me that he and Eli had owned the 916 brand and outfit but they owed money, so they sold Peter Shelly an interest in it to start with and finally sold him all of it later.

I noticed when I worked with the Clark brothers that Eli never sat down in a chair. He would squat down in a corner or at least against the wall and drink his coffee and talk, but not much talking. They had three or four sisters and all the family I ever talked to squinched their faces when they talked.

Goerge told me that he took the big platform scales out at the Whitehouse L.C. Headquarters for the Moon Ranch. The scales were there at the Moon Ranch in Walnut Groves and I used them in 1931 and 1932 while I was working there.

He said when they dug them out at the Whitehouse they found two men's skeletons and saddled horses buried under the scales. The saddles both had the initials of the men who owned them stamped on the back of the cantles. Both horses had brands on other than L.C.

George and Jack Rutland said everything looked like two men who had been working for Tom Lyons and then suddenly disappeared. Lyons had told everyone that he paid them off and they just left the country. This happened when the L.C. was having trouble with other people trying to get some of the free range that Lyons was trying to hold by force.

In 1931, CLarence Brown and I found a skeleton in the bank of Duck Creek. We found it close to the Dike cabin after a flood caused the bank to cave in. It was put in the window at Cosgrove's Hardware store in Silver City for a long while. It was not identified so it finally disappeared, no telling where.

When Jack Rutland died he was living in a bunk house with George's sons, close to his home. Jack had no money, so George had to go home and bury Jack at Gila at his own expense.

George finally moved into Silver City and worked at the courthouse. He had been going on Grand Jury duty for several years since it always paid more than ordinary wages. So that ended his cowboy days.

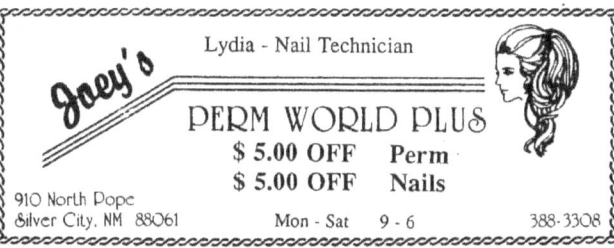

HISTORICAL OUTLOOK

TALES OF NEW MEXICO, TEXAS, AND ARIZONA

by Cecil G. Emery

Cecil Emery has lived in Grant County since 1930 except for brief spells in Arizona and Texas. He worked in the mines for 38 years. He also worked on various ranches in the area when the mines were down. It is on these ranches that he experienced all the colorful tales in his collection.

THE EMERY (PIT) FAMILY ON THE MOVE IN 1914

In March, 1914, we were living on Raggedy Creek in Foard County, three miles from Crowell, Texas when my folks made a trade. They agreed to take over some property to farm and raise stock on the plains of Texas 25 miles northeast of Lubbock and 14 miles northwest of Abernathy. The town was laid out in August, 1909 as a one section, 640 acre townsite by a group of men. One of the main men was named Abernathy, so the town was named Abernathy. It was set up next to a new railroad. The Lubbock County / Hale County line was the south line of the townsite.

We had moved so much and often that we had a chuck box with a lid that let down. It had a leg that made a table to work on while preparing a meal. It was just like the chuck wagons for cow outfits.

All of our belongings were in the wagon, including whatever blacksmith tools my father had at the time. We had a good butcher knife wheeled wagon with two big horses at the wheel and a bronc mare and bronc mule out in the lead. We had horse feed; that is, we had grain and a little hay, but mostly we staked and hobbled the horses out on grass where we camped.

There were three of us kids by then: Hazel, born in Portales, New Mexico and Nannie Bell born on Raggedy Creek, Crowell, Foard County, Texas, and me. We had to leave all our pet rabbits and other pets we had gathered up the previous fall behind and get new ones where we were going.

When we got to Pease River which was always boggy, we let the horses rest for a short while before we started across, and we made it okay.

(I remember that one of my uncles had bogged his wagon down in Pease River and had quite a time of it getting out. A cousin who was just learning to talk was very scared during this episode. Afterward, when he would see any water in the road, he would start crying and saying, "Bog a Aggie, Bog a Mule" over and over till they got away from the water.)

After we got across the river, we saw some cattle close by the water. There was a big steer that was taller than the cow he was sucking. Close by was a poor little doggie calf that was so thin that he would have to stand twice in the same place to make a shadow. My dad said, "Look at that big, old steer robbing that little calf!" I remembered that exchange all my life and saw many things that reminded me of that incident.

We climbed out of the River on just wagon tracks from four to six inches deep. It was then we saw the first car I can remember ever seeing. It did not have any top and there were three men in it. They came straight at the team, honking a horn that was pushed on a stem into the top of the door to make it operate.

When the team in the lead saw this monster and heard all this noise, they swung around and came back alongside of the wheel team, and the wheel team wanted to turn back also. The men in the monster were laughing and hollering and the team was nearly turning the wagon over.

I am sure that if my dad had time to, he would have tried to whip all three of them. From what I saw happen as I got older, I don't doubt that he could have whipped them without too much trouble. He never fought for fun, just to win. He was quite powerful and really an athlete. As it was, though, he was very busy trying to control the team and keep from getting his whole family killed.

When we got the mess straightened out, we traveled on. We went by Paducah and Matador, and then to Floydado. We rode into a snowstorm so we went into a wagon yard that had a two-eyed bachelor stove in it. It was the equivalent of a motel. The only thing in it was a bedstead and springs and bed bugs. The next morning we discovered a banty hen and her nest so we had a few eggs for breakfast.

The next morning it quit snowing. After most of it melted off, it was very cold and the wind blowing it got very muddy, so we had to stay till the second day. It was not very good then, but we went on to Abernathy anyway.

Abernathy only had a depot and about 15 houses. We went 14 miles northwest to the place we were to live. There was a lake and a lot of good grass. We had a good house there. It had ten foot ceilings which made it hard to heat, but kept it cooler in the summer.

We had a good earth tank for stock water and a place where I could bring all the mallard duck eggs and hatch them under the hens we had. They would run the old hens crazy when they would go for the water as soon as they got out of the nest. I had quail the same way.

Then I found some eggs that I did not recognize and did the same thing. When they hatched, we realized they were snake eggs! Then the hens really had a fit till my mother killed all the little snakes.

My mother, Ruby Lee, showed me how to build traps to catch all kinds of small game and quail so we nearly always had some kind of meat. What we did not need, we released.

In our pasture we could nearly always see antelope. The man who had owned it previously was a trapper and hunter. He was a taxidermist so he had all kinds of stuffed and mounted animals and birds. After he moved all his belongings away, he and some of his friends came back sometimes to hunt antelopes.

I would watch them hang up red bandana handkerchiefs and the curious antelopes would come to see the strange rags and they would kill them. We always got some of the meat. I like any meat so I thought it was good.

The first year we were at this ranch and farm we made a good crop and we got quite a bunch of all kinds of livestock as my father was a good trader. The closest neighbors were a mile away and then about three miles away.

I got my first knife by finding it near a coyote carcass. Someone had left a good knife where he had skinned the coyote, and before the day was over I had cut my finger with it.

That habit followed me most of my life. Every time I got a new knife I would cut my hand. With one new double action pistol I got, I shot the end off my left hand forefinger the first day I had it. The two forefingers match because I cut the right one off with a log and a rock while I was working for McMillen Cattle Co. Both were cut off about the back of the nail and so there is a small nail on each.

Cont'd →

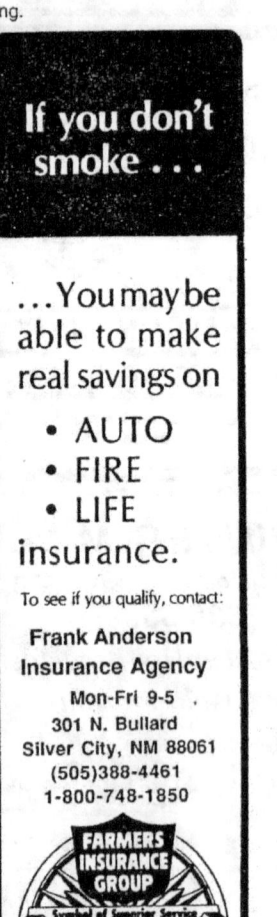

→ Cont'd

A short time after we got settled at the new place, my dad was working the wheels over on the wagon and linseed-oiling them when a family came along going on to New Mexico. They were flat broke but they had a real good four inch tire with a big team of matched horses and some of the best harness. It was really pretty with brass knobs on the hames and all the good britchen and backing straps. Everything was perfect. The family traded this for our wagon and a pair of smaller horses for $40 in cash and a little grain and fodder, and set out for New Mexico someplace.

The wagon we got was well made and nearly new. I saw 7,000 pounds hauled on it several times. It stayed with us longer than nearly anything that we ever had in those days, for my dad was a trader. I saw as many as eight head hooked to it. It made a lot of trips, short and long, before we parted with it. I believe that as many as 500 head of bronc horses and mules were broke to that wagon.

In the fall, a thrashing crew came to our place with a steam tractor to run it. It was run off coal since there was no other fuel but cowchips to burn. That was what everybody in the country used, except a little coal for special occasions if you could afford it. Until the railroad came in, all coal had to be freighted by wagon and team from Colorado City, Texas or, later, Amarillo, Texas. The wagon traveled around a hundred miles, more or less. While the thrasher was there, I had to see that everything was in order and pick up pieces of coal and put them in the bin. Next to cash, coal was the hardest thing to come by.

The man who fired the boiler for the thrasher knew that I was deathly afraid of dogs, and he could growl just like a dog. One day he jumped down by me and growled like a dog and I ran away looking back over my shoulder.

Just as I remembered there was a fence close by, I turned and hit the barbed wire with my head just above my right eye. I went through the fence and ran around the corral and stock tank to the house. I was bloody all over. It was just before noon and my mother had to stop getting dinner ready to take care of her wounded son. I was five years old at the time. When the thrashing crew came in to eat, my mother told them that she was a little late from having to tend to the wounded. The man said he did not know that I had hit the fence. He had turned and gone on about his work and did not realize what had happened. I had a big headache and fever for awhile and I still have the scar.

Some people asked me about the scar one time and I just told them that that was how close a bullet came to getting me in one of my gunfights. They thought I was very lucky.

When I was seven years old, I started school. It was seven miles with one gate and a let-down which was just a nail at the bottom of the post. Travelers masked the wires down, then crossed the wire, and then raised the wire S back up in its regular place. There were more let-downs than gates in that part of the country.

This place joined the big Spade Ranch on its east side and on the west side of our place. The horse I rode to school was a tall horse and I could not reach the stirrup. To mount, I had to tie a double rope in the fork of the saddle to put my right foot in. Then I could reach the stirrup with my left foot and get on. In the summer when I was barefoot I could straddle my toes on the horse's leg above his knee and get on from there.

I went with our closest neighbor when I was not old enough to ride by myself. Mr. Austin Vaughn would put me up behind him and take me. He had two boys, one my age and one three years older than I, but they never helped with the livestock. They hardly ever came out to help with branding or anything, but I was always there. Mr. Vaughn and I were friends for as long as he lived. He didn't think there was anything I couldn't do. Actually, I didn't have enough sense to *not* try anything that came up.

My dad and Mr. Vaughn went to Frank Norfleet's ranch and bought some old Mexican cattle together on one trip. Sometimes I would have to put out feed for them when my dad was gone at feed time. This was a risky job since these cattle would chase anyone on foot; it was their firm intention to do you bodily harm. So I had to watch out and not go any-place on foot where cattle could see me.

I had my first team run away with me when I was five years old. (I had many more in my lifetime.) I drove a team through a gate and one kicked the other one over the tongue of the wagon. It was about sundown and the team had wanted to go home at feeding time.

We sure tore up a corn patch! The corn was already ripe and it was sure making a lot of noise hitting the wagon bed!

My dad finally caught the back of the bed and got in the wagon. He had to go out on the tongue to get the lines since I had almost fallen out of the wagon bouncing over the furrows, and I had lost the lines. When my father caught the wagon to catch the team, he got a big splinter in his hand so we had to cut it out. Mr. Vaughn told me the next time I saw him that

he could hear the noise at his corral about one and a half miles away.

My brother Frank was born at this place. The doctor came from Abernathy 14 miles away. This was in the fall of 1915.

At home, we roasted peanuts and popcorn and played dominos many nights. My mother taught me to read and write. She could talk and count in both French and German. She had picked up these languages from people she was around when I started school. I could read and write and count to a hundred by ones or five or tens. She would show me how to look up words in the dictionary.

At school there was a big dictionary and I sure used it a lot. It was a one room, ten grade school. I listened to all the classes and everything that was said in the school every day, and it was all very interesting.

We had a boy of 18 staying with us in 1916. His name was Tom Turner. His dad had bought the land and the family planned to take over the ranch in the first part of 1917. During the fall of that year, old man Turner passed away. Tom set out at 1:00 a.m. for Lubbock when he got word. My dad saddled his horse for him and he set out; two hours later he was in Lubbock, 25 miles southeast of the ranch.

After he came back, Tom went to Canada to join up and fight the Germans with Canada. He went through the war and joined the U.S. troops when they arrived after the Armistice was signed.

One day Tom and a new recruit took some hand grenades to go fishing and the new man pulled the pin and kept it too long. It killed Tom, but he said Tom knocked him out of the way and saved his life.

Our cousin, Elbert Evans, was a preacher, so he became a chaplain; he went into battle and got killed. A neighbor who lived 15 miles from us was also killed in World War I.

The Turner family moved into the place we had been living in since 1914 in the first part of 1917. There was the widow and an old bachelor son, Jason, and a married son, Wheeler Turner, and a 17 year old girl and a young girl 9 years old named Floy. We were always friends. My family moved a few miles south of the original place which then became known as the Turner place.

I still went to the same school at County Line (it was built on the Lubbock and Hale county line). The one room school had an old maid teacher by the name of Miss Helms. She used a board with holes bored into it to whip kids, and a bottle of quinine with a paddle to give big kids punishment if they were too big to whip. Once was all it took to break them of breaking the rules!

One 15 year old boy, Hugh Spreister, told my dad that Miss Helms had hit him one lick and made blisters, and the next lick she just moved over a little and busted the blisters. By 1918 we had a new two room school and two teachers.

We left there in December of 1919 and went to Sterling City, Texas on the west fork of the Concho River where we bought an irrigated farm and ranch. We were on the move again, which was repeated many times, mostly by horse power and covered wagons and other horse-powered vehicles.

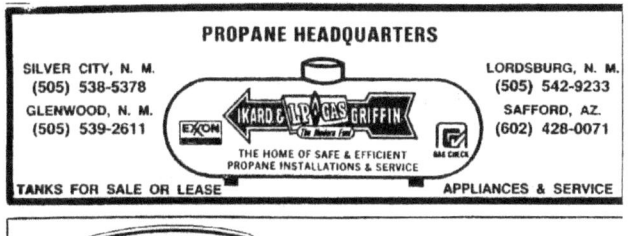

37

HISTORICAL OUTLOOK

TALES OF NEW MEXICO, TEXAS, AND ARIZONA

by Cecil G. Emery

Cecil Emery has lived in Grant County since 1930 except for brief spells in Arizona and Texas. He worked in the mines for 38 years. He also worked on various ranches in the area when the mines were down. It is on these ranches that he experienced all the colorful tales in his collection.

MY 80 YEARS OF IDEAS AND OBSERVATIONS ON THE WILDLIFE AND PEOPLE WHO INHABIT THE GOOD OLD MOTHER EARTH

There has been a lot of abuse for many years by some humans of the natural lay of the earth and some of the animals, both domestic and natural wildlife. Some of this is done through greed and some of it through ignorance.

The New Lands

This is especiallly true in so-called "new" lands, land used after it had lain fallow for centuries, occupied only by native creatures. Occasionally, humans would rove through the area hunting for enough meat to survive.

There were no fences to prevent the animals from moving to the best feed or from following the rains that kept the forage growing. As the meat animals moved, the meat-eating animals migrated with them, from season to season, for years and years.

Predator Control

In the early 1900s, the government and the only industry (ranch animals) in most of the western states kept hunters and trappers working in the most heavily predator populated areas to try to keep the lion, bear, and coyote and, in some places, even lobo wolves under control. As the deer and other wild animals were thinned out, of course, the un-thinned out meat eaters had turned to eating domestic animals in order to survive.

The counties usually paid a bounty for the most detrimental predators so that any man could get a little grocery money now and then if he chanced upon a so-called varmint.

By about 1940, most of the bounty money was cut off and a lot of out of state hunters began to come into this country as better roads were built and better (greater velocity, more efficient) ammunition was invented.

Deer Decimation Checking Station

A lot of the areas with a heavy deer population were nearly wiped out. For instance, advertisers informed hunters that the road to Beaver Head was opened up by way of North Star Mesa. A checking station was put up at the Mimbres Ranger Station and in the first year 3600 deer were checked out in a two week season. The second year they took 2800, and every year after that a lot less, till it did not pay to maintain a checking station.

Land of the Strong and the Curious

We are lucky enough to still have some wilderness area where there are no roads. Mostly just strong, young people and people with plenty of money to afford pack outfits are able to use this land. Some of this land is so rough and brushy that even the youngest and hardiest do not enter, but the deer do.

When lions and bears were left reasonably unmolested, there were times that lion tracks were thicker than deer tracks. When we were working in this country, more lions were seen than in many years. I have been on the Gila River fishing and have gone back over my trail and found lion tracks on top of my tracks. They seem to be very curious. I saw more lions and a lot more tracks than I had seen in prior years where there were hunters after them and a bounty was being paid.

Lion Traffic

The Upper Mimbres was the same way. One time I was fishing above the Figure 9 Corral when I heard some rocks roll down behind me. I looked around and a lion was looking at me. I moved over two or three feet and the she-lion headed for the water and ran. If I had not moved, she would have hit me in the back since she was lifting off the ground just as I moved. That was my only encounter with a lion, but I have had bobcats try to jump out of trees and off bluffs on me if they were crowded. Then they would just try to run and get away; that was all they wanted to do in the first place.

Predator Power

When the predators are allowed to multiply around limited game, sometimes the game become nearly non-existent. Those game not killed by predators migrated to safer territory.

One year, all the game stayed away from the range on the south side of Tadpole Ridge for four months; in the late fall, they came back. The first thing we found was fresh kills by lions. They had eaten what they wanted and covered the remains. Some were only a few hours old.

Predator Bears and Eagles

It is nearly impossible to raise any calves where bear are thick for they will catch the calves laying where the cows leave them when they go to get water the calves can't reach. If a cow happens to come to the calves' rescue, they may kill her or at least cripple her, and usually she will die soon after.

Eagles do a lot of damage, too. They get the young calves easily. They hit a grown cow in the loins and kidneys and they never get over the wounds even though they may live on for a long period before dying.

Coyotes and Calves

Coyotes will always catch a calf laying hidden out. There are at least two coyotes and they work as a team. When the calf jumps up, he will sometimes charge the intruder. When he does, the other coyote gets him from behind. The calf's tongue hangs out as he bellows, so even if the coyotes are run off the calf wil die because he can't suck. *TONGUE BIT OFF*

Usually when cattle are calving, one old cow babysits with several calves each day and they trade off so all the cows get to water at least every other day. But the babysitter cow has to graze sometime, and that's when the coyotes slip up on the calves that are furthest from her protection.

Coyotes and Turkeys

I have also witnessed coyote hunting turkey. They nearly always get their turkey. A turkey will fly and get away; but when he lands, there will be another coyote across the canyon waiting for the turkey to land. If the turkey is not too tired to fly, he may make a second flight. But when he lands again, most of the time he will land right where another coyote is positioned, and the turkey feast begins.

Cont'd →

→ Cont'd

The Domestication of the Southwest

In the first part of the 1900s, there was a lot of country that was very sparsely inhabited by human beings in the Southwest. There were just some mountains and some large plains; no one had stocked the country with livestock. The natural waters were all that could be depended on until exploraton was feasible and scarce money made available to make extra water.

Gambling with the Weather

Sometimes this was a very risky undertaking. Occasionally, a lot of livestock was put on a range where it looked like the forage would last indefinitely. But if it stayed dry for a prolonged period, all the forage would be eaten or tromped out. The feed was back too far to get to and make it back to water. Of course, the poorer the stock got, the less distance they could go to graze. At times, thousands of stock died before it would rain. Then the grasses would be eaten out, root and all. Sometimes cows would get so poor and weak they would get down and wallow around on the ground till they rubbed holes in the hide over their hip bones. The bones would be shining as big as a silver dollar. This happened to horses, too. But by some miraculous effort they would get up and reel off; when it did rain, they would get fat again.

Loco Stock

Sometimes horses and cows would get loco and live for weeks without water. I've seen horses on the flats creeping along in the mirages that happen in the flats. They would look like camels or dromedaries. After a while, they would get in close enough to smell water. They would stop and stand, and start visibly sucking and swallowing the water. Now and then, they would take a step, for loco stock cannot stand long without moving.

Sometimes they would jump eight or ten feet to get over a trail two inches deep and a foot wide. It must seem like a canyon to them. Sometimes they'd wander off away from the water before they even got into it a quarter of a mile. Some of these horses would live like this for weeks and be in such poor shape that they would have to stand twice in the same place to make a shadow.

Fire Guards

When the grass and all the other forage was eaten, there wasn't much danger in fires; most of the fires were in places that had lush growths and dry spells. Yet all over the plains of Texas, the panhandle of Oklahoma, West Kansas, Southeastern Colorado, and Eastern New Mexico (to the Pecos River), fire guards were plowed for miles to try to turn the fires or contain them. There would be two or three fire guards plowed some hundred yards apart. Some of these fire guards would stretch for 20 or more miles.

Sometimes these fire guards backfired. In the fall, after the grass was mature, all a fire needed was a still day. If you started a fire, it would make a draft and travel. Often the backfires would jump a plowed fire guard and get away and start a real fire. Sometimes a cow chip would catch fire and the wind would catch it and roll it across the country to set more fires, the same way a pine burr does in the mountains. The only difference is that a pine cone will explode when it gets real hot, and so will rocks.

Salt Water Wells and Arid Land

I have witnessed millions of acres of the same land being plowed up and wells being drilled in to irrigate. Every few years, the water table lowered and the well had to be dug deeper. Sometimes the water table sank so low that salt water came in and ruined the fertile soil.

As people keep multiplying and expanding in ever greater numbers, and less is put back in the earth than is being taken out, we kill off more land. Some of the best land is being used to stack up big buildings so that more people can be accommodated. And they have to be fed from the land that is left and the water that is being depleted day after day.

Mouths to Feed and People Power

The fact remains that people have to be fed. The people that manage to make a living and have a little left over still have to pay the bill for the unlucky. They also have to pay for the ones who think they are owed a living, regardless of whether they pull their own weight in keeping the world turning.

On the other hand, there are some that are in a position to do a lot of good for the land and leave it better off for future generations, or they can be a big detriment to all mankind and animals.

Cont'd →

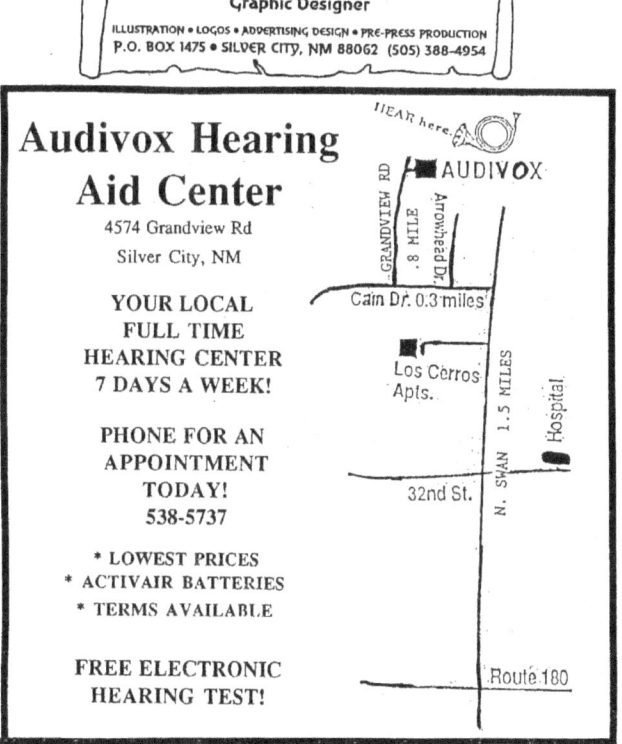

→ Cont'd

The Domestication of the Southwest

In the first part of the 1900s, there was a lot of country that was very sparsely inhabited by human beings in the Southwest. There were just some mountains and some large plains; no one had stocked the country with livestock. The natural waters were all that could be depended on until exploraton was feasible and scarce money made available to make extra water.

Gambling with the Weather

Sometimes this was a very risky undertaking. Occasionally, a lot of livestock was put on a range where it looked like the forage would last indefinitely. But if it stayed dry for a prolonged period, all the forage would be eaten or tromped out. The feed was back too far to get to and make it back to water. Of course, the poorer the stock got, the less distance they could go to graze. At times, thousands of stock died before it would rain. Then the grasses would be eaten out, root and all. Sometimes cows would get so poor and weak they would get down and wallow around on the ground till they rubbed holes in the hide over their hip bones. The bones would be shining as big as a silver dollar. This happened to horses, too. But by some miraculous effort they would get up and reel off; when it did rain, they would get fat again.

Loco Stock

Sometimes horses and cows would get loco and live for weeks without water. I've seen horses on the flats creeping along in the mirages that happen in the flats. They would look like camels or dromedaries. After a while, they would get in close enough to smell water. They would stop and stand, and start visibly sucking and swallowing the water. Now and then, they would take a step, for loco stock cannot stand long without moving.

Sometimes they would jump eight or ten feet to get over a trail two inches deep and a foot wide. It must seem like a canyon to them. Sometimes they'd wander off away from the water before they even got into it a quarter of a mile. Some of these horses would live like this for weeks and be in such poor shape that they would have to stand twice in the same place to make a shadow.

Fire Guards

When the grass and all the other forage was eaten, there wasn't much danger in fires; most of the fires were in places that had lush growths and dry spells. Yet all over the plains of Texas, the panhandle of Oklahoma, West Kansas, Southeastern Colorado, and Eastern New Mexico (to the Pecos River), fire guards were plowed for miles to try to turn the fires or contain them. There would be two or three fire guards plowed some hundred yards apart. Some of these fire guards would stretch for 20 or more miles.

Sometimes these fire guards were backfired. 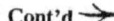 In the fall, after the grass was mature, all a fire needed was a still day. If you started a fire, it would make a draft and travel. Often the backfires would jump a plowed fire guard and get away and start a real fire. Sometimes a cow chip would catch fire and the wind would catch it and roll it across the country to set more fires, the same way a pine burr does in the mountains. The only difference is that a pine cone will explode when it gets real hot, and so will rocks.

Salt Water Wells and Arid Land

I have witnessed millions of acres of the same land being plowed up and wells being drilled in to irrigate. Every few years, the water table lowered and the well had to be dug deeper. Sometimes the water table sank so low that salt water came in and ruined the fertile soil.

As people keep multiplying and expanding in ever greater numbers, and less is put back in the earth than is being taken out, we kill off more land. Some of the best land is being used to stack up big buildings so that more people can be accommodated. And they have to be fed from the land that is left and the water that is being depleted day after day.

Mouths to Feed and People Power

The fact remains that people have to be fed. The people that manage to make a living and have a little left over still have to pay the bill for the unlucky. They also have to pay for the ones who think they are owed a living, regardless of whether they pull their own weight in keeping the world turning.

On the other hand, there are some that are in a position to do a lot of good for the land and leave it better off for future generations, or they can be a big detriment to all mankind and animals.

Cont'd →

→ Cont'd

You could see and hear them on the hunt all day long. Nothing ever stopped them.

One rainy morning, I was riding a young horse that belonged to Hank Thomas of Silver City. I did not take a rope as it would have been too stiff to throw very well. Suddenly, we came upon a buck, a big one, with several coyotes after him. He went off in a deep wash for a ways and I went after the coyotes. They turned off and circled around to get at the deer again.

The buck was pretty tired; his tongue was out and some of his ribs were showing where skin had been torn off. My horse caught the buck and put his head over my horse's back for a short distance. I pulled him off as I saw a bunch of loose horses up ahead; the young horse did not handle very well around horses at that time.

I ran the coyotes for a ways till they scattered in the brush. They were circling back to take up the chase of the buck and I'd bet they finished the job. They hardly ever left even the bones for evidence.

One morning, Emmett Fitzpatrick and I ran into a bunch of coyotes in the wet brush. We had guns so we fired one shot each, but did not connect. There were a lot of deer tracks and there was a doe and an unborn fawn there that were just about eaten up. Two hours later, we came back and there was not even any hair left. Further on we found another kill cleaned up since we were there before. We saw at least 15 coyotes. I've seen coyotes come by my house after elk and deer a good many times.

Human Prey?

One year just before Christmas when my son, Jim, was about ten years old, he went up in the Fort Bayard Reserve about five miles to hunt a Christmas tree. It was a Saturday when I was working day shift. When I came in that evening, he had not returned and had been gone most of the day. So I went up and found him about two miles above the house.

It was sundown when I got to him. He was dragging a beautiful ten foot tree but there were eight or ten coyotes all around him. Jim had a hatchet, he said, and he threw rocks at them sometimes. He had a dog with him that was a year old. He said they had followed him all the way with the tree, sometimes real close. They moved off a little when I came, but in a short time they were back. (They always seem to know when you don't have a gun.) They followed us clear to our house which was too close for comfort.

The coyotes got the dog a short time later and they only left a few yellow hairs where they ate him. When Jim got another pup that was red, they caught the pup when he was just a year old and all they left was a few red hairs. Jim also had a big tomcat that he thought a lot of and a hydrophobic skunk bit him. I had to kill him because he nearly bit Jim.

Hydrophobia

Jim did not realize that anything was wrong with the cat. I was going to pick the cat up when I noticed that something was wrong.

I have witnessed several mad (hydrophobic) animals. I saw my first mad dog when I was only four years old. You don't forget the look of the animals. When I was 15, a mad dog cut me off from everything but an old outhouse and kept me hemmed up for over an hour. When he left, he bit a cow before I could hunt him down and kill him.

At the A.T. Cross, a hydrophobic coyote came to the bunkhouse when it was hot weather and we did not have a screen door. About a dozen men were sleeping in the bunkhouse. When I woke up, the moon was shining real bright and there was a coyote standing there with his head in the open door, saliva dripping from his jaws onto the floor.

When I hollered he turned and left, but two or three men woke in time to see him. We slept with the door shut the rest of the night.

A lot of people have been bitten by hydrophobic skunks while asleep. Those who did not get the right treatment died a horrible death. I had a friend for about 14 years who got bitten and had to go to Austin, Texas and take a long series of painful shots.

Snakes

Rattlesnakes and a few other poisonous snakes may be part of the ecology, but they are definitely bad for other animals and certainly for all humans. I have seen hundreds of them in piles scattered over the Southwest, but I never got bitten. Luckily, I was careful and killed a good many that tried to bite me. I was just lucky enough to beat them to the draw. Even now, poisonous ones will make you hurt yourself when they show up unexpectedly.

Summary

I have lived with all these things and enjoyed lots of them, but these are just my ideas and not necessarily anyone else's.

I do not believe in ruining the land. Pollution should be curtailed as much as possible to try to keep every living thing as healthy as possible.

We also need to feed and take care of our population on the earth and the animals that are here and a part of the world. I've never killed anything that I could not eat except skunks and rattlesnakes.

I like to fish but I never waste fish. If I did not like the fish I would not catch them. I do not believe that anything should be wasted because I think that a family might be made destitute by waste. It goes on up to a whole nation. Waste can defeat the strongest nation in the world -- the good old U.S. of America.

OPEN FORUM   Cont'd From Page 11

in New Mexico -- the list includes the grizzly bear, the black-footed ferret, and the jaguar.

We have the chance to undo some of the wrongs we have committed against the wolf. Wolves belong in the wild in New Mexico. Bring Back the Lobo!
Sincerely,
Dr. Susan Larson
P.S. I am not alone in my sentiments. A recent poll conducted by the NM Game & Fish Dept. showed that the public supports wolf reintroduction by a *2 to 1* margin in New Mexico.

To express your support, write to:
Manuel Lujan, Secty. of Interior
Department of Interior
18 & C Streets NW
Washington, DC 20240
Ed. Note - Along with being a veterinarian, Susan Larson is also chairperson of the Mexican Wolf Coalition and a member of the Sierra Club Wildlife Commission.

RESPONSE TO SACRED COWS
by Cecil Emery

This is a response to a Mr. Lee Woods of one of the lower states (Louisiana); it specifically responds to the so-called cow pollution of the water in streams on the Frisco River and other territories and his references to the cow piles.

The piles are only composted vegetation. If he is truly a vegetarian, it would not poison him if he ate a little of it. I don't say it would taste good.

I never ate any animal dung intentionally, but anyone who has worked with livestock has accidentally tasted some of it and it never hurt them.

I have seen all kinds of canines eat fresh cow and horse dung so it must be something they need in their diet.

Of course, fowl and hogs will clean up after cows and horses. Since it's only composted vegetation, it still has some food value.

The droppings of vegetation eating animals are the best natural fertilizer in the world. It will rebuild the soil depletion faster than any fertilizer known. Human waste will pollute water and land and fill it with diseases more than any animal waste.

The cows were put here the same as all other animals. The most authentic book that has ever been printed (the Bible) spells out that they were for human consumption just like vegetation to make a balanced diet.

I have also seen fresh cow dung used to heal wounds and draw large thorns out of human flesh. (Of course, when you can get something better, you should do so.)

I have drunk some water that had a good percent of cow droppings and it was wet. I have also watched the Apache Indians eat many of the entrails of animals. All they did was strip the guts between their fingers to clean the green stuff out and then they cooked them a little, not much. I never knew of any of them getting sick and I know that the taste had to still be there.

STOP RATTLESNAKE ROUNDUPS!

Rattlesnakes are sentient beings with an important place in the predator/prey (rodents and other small mammals) relationship.

Most of the rattlesnakes are captured by spraying gasoline into their dens during hibernation, which kills other animals as well.

Autopsies performed on rattlers after they were gassed revealed severe lung damage, pneumonia, and tissue deterioration.

The gasoline prevents other animals from using the area for denning and hibernation. It can also pollute underground water.

To control the overpopulation of rodents caused by these roundups, pesticides are used which further pollute the environment.

The roundups have caused great suffering and environmental damage in Texas and Oklahoma, and now organizers want to exploit New Mexico.

We *must stop* rattlesnake roundups from becoming established in this state.

Kick off Earth Week (April 22-28) with a productive and legal **protest**.

HELP WANTED
The Wilderness Outlook is looking for display ad salespeople in all areas! Must be environmentally concerned. Willing to make a full-time effort for a part-time position. Experience helpful-not necessary. Send resume to 503 N. Bullard, Silver City, NM 88061

When: April 21 from 10 - 6 or as long as you stay
Where: Otero Cty. Fairgrounds
401 Fairgrounds Rd.
(off White Sands Blvd.)
Alamogordo, NM
Bring water and your own sign. Some slogans for signs might be:
DON'T TREAD ON ME!
STOP THE HERPICOST!
STOP RATTLESNAKE RIPOFFS!
ROUNDUPS KILL MORE THAN SNAKES!
PROTECT ALL WILDLIFE!
DRINK YOUR GASOLINE!

For more information, write to: Bob Young, *Sangre de Cristo Animal Protection, Inc.*, P. O. Box 2153, Las Cruces, NM 88004. Bob can be reached by phone at 505-382-7140 or 505-526-6041.

ADC DELAYS TRAP RETRIEVAL

The Animal Damage Control division of the U.S. Department of Agriculture on the NMSU campus is in the business of trapping and poisoning predators in Southern New Mexico at the requests of farmers and ranchers.

Division trappers are only required to check their traps twice a week. This means that trapped animals (often badly injured) must sometimes endure three or four days of severe stress without food and water before finally being slaughtered by the trapper or another animal.

In a recent letter to me, a USDA official stated " ... It is not in ADC's best interest to prolong retrieval. The longer an animal is trapped, the more likely it is to escape, and an injured predator poses an increased threat to livestock."

Then why don't they check their traps daily?

In the last reply from the same official "...While we understand your feeling about this situation, we do not believe any change in our operations is warranted." In other words, the USDA is not concerned about the welfare of predators (or livestock) caught in their traps.

This is the same federal agency charged with enforcement of the Animal Welfare Act which continues to completely ignore the care of farm animals, birds, and rodents used in biomedical research.
Bob Young
Sangre de Cristo
Animal Protection, Inc.

TALES OF NEW MEXICO, TEXAS, AND ARIZONA

by Cecil G. Emery

Cecil Emery has lived in Grant County since 1930 except for brief spells in Arizona and Texas. He worked in the mines for 38 years. He also worked on various ranches in the area when the mines were down. It is on these ranches that he experienced all the colorful tales in his collection.

THE FOREVER LOST COWBOY

In the fall of 1937, I was at the G.O.S. Ranch. At that time, Hub Estes had a chance to sell some horses to the Diamond Bar Ranch.

Bob Steele was the foreman for the ranch there, and he sent him about 30 head of extras that he had traded for. Nearly all of them had been tried out at the G.O.S. before he got the order for the horses.

There were no top horses in the bunch, but all were serviceable horses. Bob was in need of horses and paid for them so he could use them immediately. We did not hear much comment about what they thought of the horses for quite a while as everybody was busy working cattle on both ranches.

One day Hub ran into Bob Steele in Silver City when Bob was nearly through gathering the cattle and shipping them. He told Hub he was going to have to lay off some men. Hub was looking for a couple of men to work at the G.O.S., so Bob sent two men down to the ranch about four days later. One of the men was Frank Ferguson who had been raised on the Mimbres River. I had worked with him in the mines in Miami, Arizona. Frank was a good man but he did not like to ride much. He asked Hub if he could have the farm job at the headquarters. He got it and stayed for three or four years.

The other man that came was named Jack Rossi who said he was a Frenchman. Jack had the best-looking cowboy rigging and clothes I've ever seen. It was so correct that a cowboy catalogue could have used him for advertisement.

Jack had been in several western states, he said, punching cattle. He probably had, as I doubt that he stayed long at any one outfit based on what happened at the G.O.S. Ranch after he came there.

It was about night when he arrived at the camp on the Sapillo at the old Goforth Place (it's the Gila River Ranch now). We were in a little side canyon in some big pine trees. The pack boxes were stacked against a big tree with the pack covers over them for protection from weather and varmints. We had a cook fire right close and had our Dutch ovens and coffee pot out.

Close by camp, each man would put his pallet, or hot roll, down, with the head uphill if the ground was uneven, which most of the time was the case. The first thing Jack did was roll out his bed with the foot uphill.

After we were through supper and we were ready to go to bed, Jack just squatted down to relieve himself! When I hollered at him to get out of camp, he said he would get lost in the dark. I told him he would get worse than lost if he ever tried a thing like that again. One or two more of the men told him plenty after that when they realized what was taking place.

All night he kept sliding downhill out of his bed because he had it turned wrong. When we got up the next morning, had breakfast, and went to saddle up, I noticed that Jack had one of the heaviest saddles I ever saw (it weighed about 65 pounds). He said it had a double, rawhide-covered, 17 inch tree made from the heaviest bullhide leather. There were heavy leather taps (tapederos - long ears) on it, too. He had the longest, shanked bits, all silver mounted, and a high curb. To complete the look, he had big, silver-mounted spurs, and heavy, bullhide chaps (chapaderos), bugger-red pants, and a jacket. I was young and fairly strong, but I could just barely pick up the saddle. When he put the saddle on a horse and got on with all that rigging, that horse was loaded up.

When we got started on the drive to work cattle, he decided he had to have a bowel movement. He asked me to wait or he would be lost. Afterward, every time we got out of his sight, he would start squalling like a panther that he was lost.

In the brush, you don't see anyone very far apart, but you do have to spread out to work any country in the mountains. Of course, it *is* hard to do anything if you have to take care of another man all the time. You might just as well be riding the same horse, or, better, just leave him in camp. This went on for a few days.

One day before we left the camp at the Goforth Place, we went up from the mouth of No Name Canyon toward the bridge where the highway crosses Sapillo Creek below the Goforth place. The canyon is bluffed up for a few miles; it also stays froze up in the winter time so we had to go up quite a ways together before we could spread out to work the cattle out of the brush.

As we rode along, Jack said he had a belly ache and had to stop, but nobody stopped. He kept coming along until finally I smelled something. I looked down at the bottom of Jack's pants legs and saw that his bowels had emptied and were running out. He complained that nobody would stop and he would get lost if he stopped by himself. I told him that he could not get out of the canyon till he got to the head of it. It was too cold to stop, but he got down, undressed, and washed up with liquid ice. Then he put his wet, frozen clothes back on and we went on our way. That was a stinking mess! We just had him follow someone that day, and if he got out of sight, he would holler he was lost.

When Hub came down, we moved up to the Biddle Place with what stock we were holding to work gathering some more stock. The Biddle Place was where Lake Roberts is now. At that time, there was a spring, an old log cabin, and a set of corrals there. We gathered all the cattle and the mules up on the Biddle pasture. After we got them separated, we drove the other mules and the mare and colt, and they kept trying to break away.

One went out by Jack so Hub was hollering at Jack to head them off. The old horse went through the saplings and oaks and he headed the mule off. Jack was hollering, "Someone catch my horse! He's running away!" Hub told Jack, "That's the best I ever seen you do!" Hub had noticed the long shanked bits on Jack's bridle and told him to tie his reins in the nose band. He had on his bridle headstall and if the reins had not been real

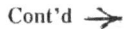
Cont'd ➙

→ Cont'd

stout he would have broken them in the race. The horse brought the mule back and Jack was pretty well skinned up. The old horse was tender-mouthed but real high-headed. He would have made a good horse to hunt flying geese on. We moved to the ranch that day and never had any more incidents. Hub used to come around to Jack Rossi every now and then and praise him for the good job he had done turning the mule.

When we got to the ranch, Hub put Jack to cutting wood one day and he could not even do that. Hub told him he did not need him any longer. Then Hub told me that Bob Steele must have been trying to get even with him because of some of the horses he had pawned off on Bob. A few months before at the Diamond Bar Ranch, it sort of led me to think that the two had a few words on the subject.

I know I have worked with some people that were of French extraction, but Jack Rossi was the only one that ever told me he was a Frenchman from France. He said he had worked in several western states as a cowboy and had moved around considerably, I imagine mostly by request. He probably hauled his outfit around more than he rode it, especially in the mountains.

I saw Jack Spruil riding this same high-headed horse in the elk pasture. He was running a bunch of steers and the old horse would not turn or stop, so just as he got to the big juniper, he just jerked the horse's head and hit the big juniper and uprooted the tree. He finally wound up going over the tree. The old horse could not straighten his neck out for several days.

He also scared a bunch of elk down on the north hillside. One old elk cow slid under my horse's belly and went on down the hill. The old horse I was riding humped up and was afraid to move. I think my puckering string drew up two or more notches. Anyway, we did not have a wreck and several years later the old, dead juniper was still in the saddle in the elk pasture.

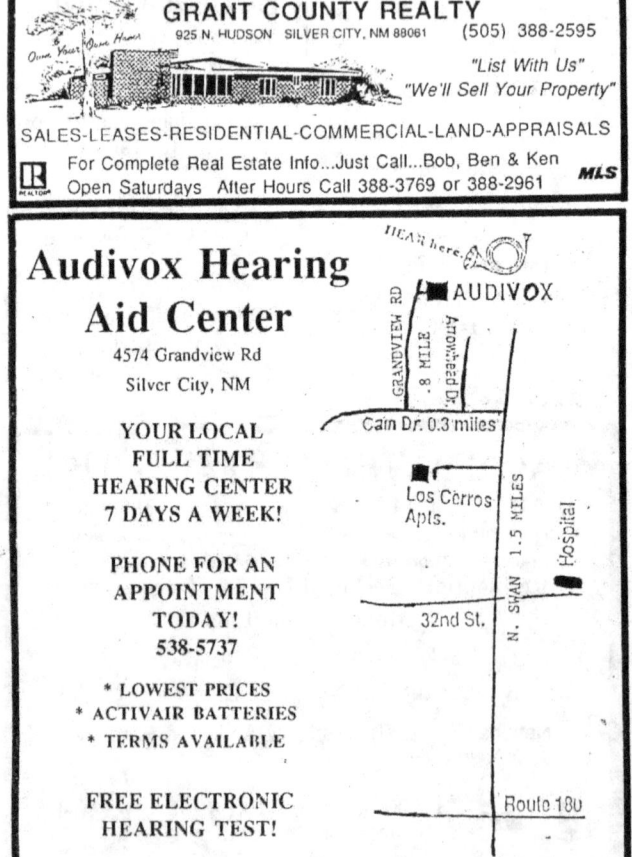
A VOICE FROM 1930

In February, 1990, the following letter was found in a glass jar stored inside a rock pillar at 375 Racetrack Road. This property now belongs to Jack Green, son of Forest Green, who bought the property from the author, E.C. White, in 1940. It was typed on paper with a letterhead that reads: Valley View Ranch, Rancho del Valle de Buena Vista, E.C. White, P.O. Box 204, Central, NM.

To Future Generations of Men:

This epistle is being written on the second day of July, 1930; it will be placed within a bottle in a stone fence built by the hand of E.C. White on his property, located one and a half miles southwest of Central, New Mexico, United States of America.

We have often reflected on what future generations will be like; namely, in way of thought. We wonder if you will not laugh at our poor intelligence of this age. This is, as you know, the fast age; the age of worship of the golden Calf; the age of Crime; an hysterical age devoid of reason; the age of force, a force you use to get what you want no matter what methods must needs be resorted to in doing so. (This is) an age still under the dominating lash of religious influence.

A man must have overwhelming nerve, or gall, to assert his opinions in public on religion, politics, or economics. A few chosen ones, chosen by whom we do not know, control all the financial influence, control all thought of the people, control everything, as it were, for their own personal financial gain. Everything is done in this age for money; nothing for benefit of mankind --- only in rare exceptions. A few sufferers of the Great World War are still bleeding out their hearts for mankind, but what can they do?

Should a conscientious newspaper editor or a district attorney cry out against the existing criminal conditions, he is usually boycotted, or shot, by the politico-criminal element. Let anybody dare criticize any one of the hundred warring factions of the present day religious sects, with all their glamorous display of God influence, and you are called atheist and are shunned by human society.

Most of the great teachers and other supposed human benefactors are a lot of propagandists and fanatical reformers, rigorously trying to cram down peoples' throats with force their own pet beliefs, usually for their own personal financial gain. This is the tenth year of prohibition in the United States, and as much or more drinking is going on than at any other time in the history of the nation. Bootleggers and preachers of the holy gospels are dictating public affairs, if not directly, indirectly.

A group of flannel-mouthed, fickle-minded censors are dictating, with their own narrow viewpoints on matters, the moral code and methods of living in this country, yet hatreds, famines, and sufferings are prominent in everyday news. Several million men are starving in the United States at this writing, yet our great political bodies are out fishng, or lounging about a summer resort.

The churches are still collecting money from the poor and needy so that the ministers, priests, and other lazy grafters can get fat. A small estimate of what is shipped from the United States each year to the Vatican in Rome would be up in the billions of dollars, yet we're going hungry.

When a man loses all ambition for self-respectful work, he takes up preaching. It is an easy living. Even some of our ex-stage people who have learned the powers of speech have gone into the ministerial alliance,

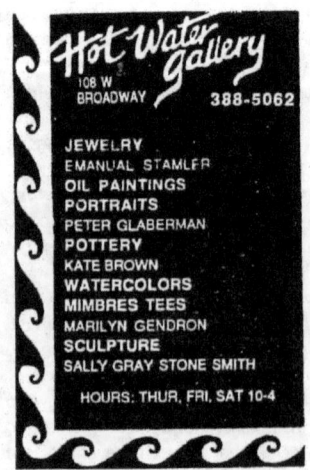

TALES OF NEW MEXICO, TEXAS, AND ARIZONA

by Cecil G. Emery

Cecil Emery has lived in Grant County since 1930 except for brief spells in Arizona and Texas. He worked in the mines for 38 years. He also worked on various ranches in the area when the mines were down. It is on these ranches that he experienced all the colorful tales in his collection.

AUNT LOU PIPER: COMANCHE INDIAN

In October of 1931, I was working over at Pine Cienega close to Carlisle near the border of New Mexico and Arizona when an old fellow told me that an old campsite there had been occupied by a Commanche Indian woman by the name of Lou Jones.

Lou Jones had two children, a boy and a girl, who were red-headed. She had asked Tom Johnson if she could milk some of the range cows that were running in that part of the LC range (Tom Lyons and Cambell ranch. Tom Johnson was wagon boss for the LC.)

Tom told Lou to help herself and later they went by the camp and Lou had over 20 head of old range cows with their calves in a corral she had built. She would leave the calves in the corral in the daytime, then milk the cows and let the calves outside to graze at night. She always left behind part of the milk for the calves.

Lou sold milk and butter to a sawmill crew a couple of miles off towards Carlisle. She stayed till she had enough money to move on. When she left she had two horses with travois and her two kids and all her belongings.

In 1935, I went to Central Heights, Arizona to work which was halfway between Miami and Globe. When I got there, I began to hear of Aunt Lou Piper. I got acquainted with an old time cowman who was an old friend of John Watson (my wife's father). This man told me that this Lou Piper came there with two children, a boy and girl by the name of Jones, and quite a while later married Piper.

This man said there had been a lot of unbranded cattle and, of course, the calves got big without being branded. He said Lou got more than her share of all of them till she had a large ranch built up of at least 3,000 head of mother cattle. She did not own enough land to run that many head, so when others bought up the extra land she was finally squeezed out till she only had about 400 head left. Her son had a ranch some miles away from his mother, but still in the vicinity of Miami.

It turned out that John Watson had known Lou (Jones) Piper in Pine Cienega in New Mexico. After I had been there about a year, I got acquainted with Lou Piper and her son, Jones, but I never got acquainted with her daughter.

I was told by three or four men not to try working for Lou -- that she would not pay what she owed a man. But Lou Piper needed some one to brand out her calf crop and I was fresh out of a job, so I went up to work for her.

She had a young boy there who could do pretty well what he was told to do, but he really wasn't a cowboy. The country was fairly rough and certainly brushy. We were about four days gathering and branding the calves and I found out she could do anything, although she did not ride anymore. She was better than 70 years old by then, but she still knew every cow she owned, and she knew when I had missed or left some out. But when I told her some cow had a calf too young to travel, that was okay.

Lou's son, Jones, came over while I was branding and he said his mother was sort of hard to get along with.

After the branding was over, she wanted me to stay

Cont'd ⟶

→ Cont'd

steady with her. She wanted my wife, Ruth, to come and live there, too, and help her but that did not work out.

Lou's husband, Piper, had departed a short time before I started working for Lou, so she told me the story behind their marriage and how he left.

Mr. Piper came to Globe riding a freight train with threadbare clothes. Lou said the seat of his pants were out. But he was a good miner and he got a job and came to be a mine shifter or boss.

When they got married everything ran smoothly for some time, but then Piper sort of got to laying out with the dry cows. Finally, he did not come back home for several days.

The mines had imported some Bohemians (or "Bohunks" as they were called) by the train load to keep the miners in line and break up any strike talk, for they could do anything with the Bohemians. Miami Copper did not see that these men had any housing, so most just camped out under the trees. Most bought horses, so Piper told the Bohunks that he had an old Indian squaw who would feed them and they could put their horses in her pasture.

So about 20 of the Bohunks went up about six miles to the ranch and came in after turning the horses loose. They told Lou that they were there to eat and that Piper had told them it would be okay.

Well Lou got out her old 45 pea shooter and fired a few shots close enough to put fear into all the Bohunks.

In a few days, Piper came home and she put him to flight with a good pair of pants with a seat in them. She told him that that was more than he had when he first got there. He never showed up anymore.

Then she told of the time when she was living in Pine Cienega, milking the cows to sell milk and butter to the sawmill crews while she raised two small children. She also told me how she rode long hours and months building up a herd, but later on she just had a small bunch left because she was too old to get any more back.

I told her Tom Johnson was buried in the Pinal Cemetery by Central Heights but she already knew when he died and where he was buried. She paid me what she owed me when I left and told me to come back to see her. I never did.

Her ranch house was in the head of Pinal Canyon east of Miami and Globe.

I would, at this point, however, consider moving away somewhat from the aforementioned "down home" remedies and consider "Tagamet" or, better yet, a little conversation wth the family M.D.

There is no compelling reason why you should not pursue the "spicy life"....

No restaurant today worth its salt fails to provide a hand crank pepper mill fueled with delightful Jova beads. The little mustard seed has come a long way and now is offered in hundreds of prepared variations. Bottled steak sauces abound -- you have a choice of thousands. I recommend my favorite, *Sauce Robert*, brainchild of my old friend, Chef Auguste d'Escoffier.

Vinegar -- it comes natural and distilled. If you choose the former, be *en garde* for the "mother " -- remove and discard. Many flavored types of this ol' standby are now available,

including red or white wine base, tarragon etc. -- stick to the *au natural*, but watch that mother!

Let's hear it for ketchup -- American's all-time French fry camouflage!

In Beantown, a fast man could half fill a water glass with ketchup, fill it with water at the bubbler, mix the water and ketchup, and consume it before he made a rapid exit pursued by the manager! Anyone for cold tomato soup?

Years ago most every home dining room table was graced by a "lazy Susan." Dad was always granted the first spin. It had five cut outs for salt, pepper, oil, vinegar, and mustard cruets. The device was inspired by a lack of any maid table service, in particular, one whose name was Susan.

In all of this, I've forgotten which you threw over your shoulder to ward off bad luck -- was it salt or the maid?

There are many hot sauce also- rans but only one "Tabasco" prepared by the McIllhenny family from peppers grown on an island off Louisiana.

Why an island? If these peppers were grown on the mainland, the plants' acetic transference via the soil "takes over" on neighborhood vegetables. Some mainland foks claim they still wind up with "hot" carrots - the hotness was transferred from the McIlhenny peppers on the island. True.

I personally am not an ultra high octane sauce devotee -- but, if this nectar turns you on -- get after it!

Hot sauce over-indulgence warning signs are:
1. Vertigo -- dizziness, followed by a five degree list, either to starboard (no problem) or port -- call the doctor!
2. Somnambulent tendendies -- cut back coffee intake to ten cups per day.

Welcome to the wide world of continuous condiment consumption! Lift your horizons, find new vistas to conquer, eliminate your fun threshold, tighten up your chutzpah, and loosen up your cholesterol --all aboard!

THE MOGOLLON MOUNTAINS

by Dick Hays

Back in the snow-clad mountains
The towering Mogollons
Back in the tall rim-rocks
The mountain lion roams

Back where snow lies deepest
Untouched by sun's bright beams
Back where life is born
To the roaring mountain streams

Back where the rocky peaks
Reach up to a crystal sky
Back where the fleecy clouds
Go slowly driftin' by

Back where mansanita thickets
Blanket the mountainsides
Back where the black-tail deer
Feed up on the high divides

Back where pin squirrels chatter
From the tops of tall pine trees
Back where the eagles scream
Comes driftin' on th' breeze

Back where black bear sleep
The long cold winter out
Back where the rushing streams
Are filled with speckled trout

Back were the ol' doe suckles
Her spindle-legged fawn
Back where the coyote howl
Comes mournfully with the dawn

Back where scenes are perfect
By the light of the rising sun
Back were nature's proud
Of all the things she's done

Back in the deep, dark canyons
I long to make my home
Among the snow-capped peaks
In the towering Mogollons

TALES OF NEW MEXICO, TEXAS, AND ARIZONA

by Cecil G. Emery

Cecil Emery has lived in Grant County since 1930 except for brief spells in Arizona and Texas. He worked in the mines for 38 years. He also worked on various ranches in the area when the mines were down. It is on these ranches that he experienced all the colorful tales in his collection.

BILL (CLARENCE) JOHNSON
ON MONUMENT RIDGE DRIVE

The G.O.S. outfit was camped on the Mimbres River at the Cooney place. They were working cattle out in all different directions, and when we got all the cattle worked that we could reach handy from there, we would move to another location to work. We went out to the head of Monument Canyon to work back down from Monument Park, right up against the Continental Divide.

It's a lot prettier there than at the City of Rocks, but it cannot be seen very far on account of the terrain being mostly up edgewise.

I went off down a canyon that came out a short ways below the end of Monument Ridge and picked up what cattle I found and made a holdup for the other men to throw into. It was misting and the thickening fog made voices and noises of any kind very clear. I could hear the men talking and the rocks rolling and the brush popping. The cattle I was holding got very nervous and wanted to take off.

From what I could hear, I could tell the other men had some cattle that were getting a little trotty as the country is a little weedy coming off into the Mimbres River. Finally I heard enough to know that a race was on. Some one hollered that a big steer was turning off a point that would dodge the holdup. I could tell Bill Johnson and Manuel Duran were after something (Manuel was a rep of Harry Mattocks working with us).

When they came off in the river and started going on up the river, Bill hollered, "Manuel, catch him, he's got my saddle!" I heard Manuel say he was after him and before long he had caught the steer.

When they all came in to the holdup and everything quieted down, I found out what took place.

Bill was only 15 years old and he wanted to put his rope on everything. Hub Estes had him riding some good horses that could carry him up to the lead but Bill was riding a little saddle that was not built for heavy roping. When he roped the two year old steer, the old horse stopped and Bill's little saddle went off over the horse's head. It eventually pulled off both of the horse's front shoes as the steer and saddle took off up the canyon with Manuel in pursuit.

When the saddle went over the horse's head it also pulled the horse's bridle off. He was loose but gentle so Bill caught him and got his bridle back on without much trouble. Manuel caught the steer without much trouble either. The saddle was swinging around on the end of the rope and finally it caught around a sapling and stopped the steer, so both the steer and the saddle were saved for the day. After that, Bill wasn't quite so anxious to use his rope for a while.

About three weeks before that, we were working with Will Laney up on the Heart Bars above Sycamore Canyon on some ridges called Shiprock. About 15 men with some dogs were working cattle there. We had quite a bunch of cattle and they were pretty salty so we had a lot of trouble getting them to hold up.

At one point, we couldn't get them out of a big thicket. Finally, one old G.O.S. steer broke out and made a run to go out through a saddle. He came out on the side where Clarence and I were. I was riding a big horse that was about 15 1/2 hands tall so I got up by the side of the steer and whipped him over his nose with my rope to try to turn him, but the steer was taller than my horse! Bill was staying in the lead on the same horse he had that day on Monument Ridge and trying to turn the steer from up there. Suddenly, a big walnut tree came up. I couldn't duck, but the steer went under it, so I turned back up the hill.

Bill laid down on the side of his horse on the hillside but a big, long limb caught on his saddle horn; it was about 20 feet long by the time he came out from under it. "Which way did he go?" he cried; he had his rope down to catch the steer.

I told him the steer went over the top of the ridge and I let him go. He wanted to catch him so I told him the steer was bigger than his horse and, besides, his saddle was too light for that big of an animal. We went back to the rest of the men and tried to get the cattle to move out, but

when the bunch came out, nothing would turn.

There were about 80 head all told, including about 15 head of big maverick bulls and other younger mavericks. Everything got away but 17 cows! We roped and sidelined and took off into the river toward a corral above the mouth of Sycamore Canyon. It was dark when we got them in the corral and took the sidelines off.

Will and Lawrence were camped close by, but the rest of us were camped several miles down the river at the mouth of the Sapillo. Our group included Jack Hooker and Slim Daniels, Pinky and Don Norris, and the whole G.O.S. crew which was seven men. We had to get supper and get night horses after we got to camp. It was late by then so it was not long till breakfast the next morning.

We went out to work on the Granny benches on the west side of the Gila River next. After working with Will Laney for a few days, we got the big steer that got away from Bill and me that day. We held him and got him to the Biddle holding pasture but he died; he had melted the tallow running so hard and far. I could tell he was quite old by the wrinkles way out on his horns. He was quite shelly, too.

Incidentally, Will Laney caught most of the cattle that got away that day on Battle Ship Ridge. They went out over the little Creek about 15 miles where he had some triggers set in a trap there. He told me that one of the maverick bulls gutted a good horse that he had been riding the day we worked with him.

In the G.O.S. crew at that time was Redwolf (Charlie) Hudson, Clint Johnson Jr., Clarence Johnson, Pete Beasly, myself, and two new hands from Deming. One's first name was Buck but I can't remember the other one at all for they did not stay but about one week and they quit. They said it was too weedy for them. It was just as well, for up there they were like two good men gone anyway. They hardly filled a hole, but maybe would have filled them in if they were on the flats.

The Biddle place was where Lake Roberts is now, but the pasture was north at another Biddle place where an old lumber house was once built many years ago. The one at the lakesite was a log house that had some good pole corrals.

Clarence made a good hand. He was always ready to go.

efforts of musical luminaries (from 5 -- 500 candlepower) of past, present, and future popularity.

Be you a Mozart worshiper or simply a fan in the deep water end of the pool -- this is for you!

Priced at only $7.95 per disc (no charge for delivery), you can be the first one on your block to receive EVERYTHING the "Little Master" ever penned on 180 compact discs. Don't reach for your pencil -- the total price for ALL is only $1,431. (I worked it out with my abacus beads).

Housed in their hard plastic containers (the industry refers to them as "jewel cases"), they will roost on six running feet of shelving. Start building now before lumber prices escalate.

Once you get all 180 discs aboard (it will take 15 months), you can invite all your friends over for a "Wolf-In" and spin all 180 circles for them. Before you mail the invitations, however, you'd better stack up on groceries and bed rolls; my beads tell me that even if you listen for 8 hours every day, it will still take 22 1/2 days to play it all!

After consulting both my abacus and prayer beads, I find that I can finagle my way aboard this golden purchase opportunity by taking the following stringent measures:

1. Furlough my secretary for 22 days (a la forthcoming plans by the administration for civil service employees), thus gaining a savings of $22.

2. Obtain a second mortgage on my furniture, including my C.D. player: $275.

3. Sale of Yum-Yum, my half-blind, 13 year old, constant companion Pekingese: $5.

4. Sell my 1923 Essex (runs good): $600.

5. Sale of *Avon* glass vehicle collection (some boxed) $300.

6. Wife's sale of handmade stuffed gooses at $10 each -- estimate gross sales over 15 month period (14 gooses x 10) = $210.

7. Sale of *Countess Mara*, broad width, pure silk neck ties (most without soup stains) for $1 each -- $19.

The total : $1,431.

No problem! I'll order today!

My only hesitancy is the lack of a charge card. Is this an oversight or a direct hit on us non-card carriers. I smell discrimination here! The same company honors my checks via their Compact Disc Club! I'll have to consult with my attorney!

Attention all music lovers: The big swing to compact discs has left record and tape companies in great disrepair. *Discounts abound on this fare, I go for C.D.s -- no wear, No tear, and quality to spare Let the buyer beware.*

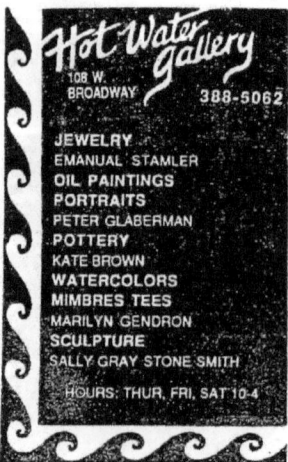
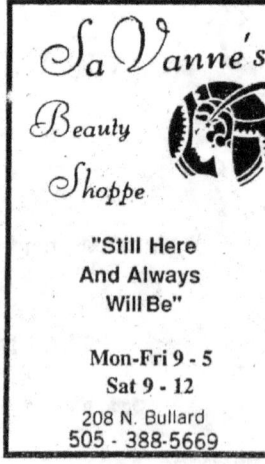
TALES OF NEW MEXICO, TEXAS, AND ARIZONA
by Cecil G. Emery

Cecil Emery has lived in Grant County since 1930 except for brief spells in Arizona and Texas. He worked in the mines for 38 years. He also worked on various ranches in the area when the mines were down. It is on these ranches that he experienced all the colorful tales in his collection.

FLOYD PROCTOR FROM CORONA, NM

When I first knew Floyd Proctor he had a sheep and cattle ranch southeast of Corona NM. He and his wife had a large family of mostly boys who were already grown and out on their own. Floyd also drove a school bus into Corona from the ranching country, so when the school bus convention was on in Silver City he would come down with his wife. They were friends of my uncle Monty Bussey and Aunt Tela, so when they tried camping and it rained, they came and stayed at my house and we got acquainted.

My son Gary Emery was in the 4-H Club then and he chose sheep as his project. Floyd Proctor had lots of fine sheep. When his sons were in 4-H they would win year after year at Roswell Cotton Carnival Fair and at the State Fair in Albuquerque. Several other boys around that part of the state kept winning after his sons were out of the competition.

Floyd gave Gary three especially good lambs so Gary and I went over to the Proctor Ranch and visited for a couple of days. He showed me a lot of country and I saw more deer than I had ever seen in any vicinity besides the north rim of Grand Canyon and Prior Mesa above the Gila Cliff Dwellings, and in North Star Mesa on the G.O.S. ranch a long time back.

The Proctor Ranch was fenced to keep coyotes out; it was also heavily trapped for bobcats and any other sheep-killing varmints. This caused the deer to multiply till they got overstocked. Then they got diseased. They had to kill two or three truckloads to thin out the diseased deer, but they were still dying off.

Floyd also had some half-breed lambs from some exotic sheep some neighbor rancher had imported from Asia. The exotic sheep would jump over into Floyd's pasture and breed these big lambs that were nearly twice as tall as regular sheep. The rancher would pay Floyd a good price for all the big lambs that were born; he would just eat them since their wool was not very good.

All the wells on Proctor's ranch were very deep so he would have to haul water out to some of the back side places to use the range. At one place where he had a lot of slick rock country and a bluff that ran some distance, he built a large steel reservoir. I believe it was 80 feet across and 8 feet high up against the bluff. He put a top on the tank to keep down evaporation; the tank top had an opening so that any additional water that fell on the top would drain into the tank.

Directly over the top of the tank, Floyd apexed a v-shaped pass. He built a metal smokestack affair out from the tank top with big flair wings that reached to the top of the bluff. Then he built a concrete wing to the flume to channel the water into the tank. When it rained, the tanks would fill up with water. To control the water, he had knee tubs with floats. There were high troughs for cattle and low troughs for sheep.

This system allowed him to use country he had only used part time before. He said he never ran out of water after he installed this waterworks.

There were lots of old Indian diggings in this part of the country so Proctor had many arrowheads and other artifacts which he fixed up in very attractive designs.

Floyd had a contract with some pharmaceutical company for 500 pounds of live rattlesnakes each year at $1 a pound. He would catch them and put them in an old galvanized water tank till he got enough, then he would let the company know and they would pick them up.

One year he had about 380 pounds of snakes gathered when a late freeze came and killed all the snakes in the tank so he had to start over. Snakes do not survive in cold weather unless they can den up.

Floyd said he had never caught but one rattlesnake over five feet long in all the years he was catching them. But I have killed several as long as

Cont'd →

six feet. I have seen some that would be even longer than that if they were hung up by the head or tail. When their muscles are relaxed they are longer; as long as they are alive, they contract their muscles and look shorter.

For several years, Floyd and his wife came to see us when the bus convention was on. He helped my son Gary to shape up the sheep and he really knew how to shear them pretty. But when Gary went to Cliff, the judges went straight to what came from Pacific Western Cattle Company, a subsidiary of Phelps Dodge. The judges awarded the blue ribbon to the boy who had the right stock from the right people.

It turns out the boys from "Pacific Switch" were showing each other's stock and the judges never knew what was going on. The first thing they switched was hogs. They got such a kick out of what they had put over, they did the same on calves and sheep. They had a good laugh out of it. But the Proctor sheep that won first and second prize at the Roswell and Albuquerque fairs did not get a notice at Cliff.

We had a lot of good mutton that fall, a little high priced since they had been fed and raised as show animals. We also had a lot of extra tallow to trim since fat is what gives show animals their well-rounded shape. I don't believe fat needs to be attached to any meat to make it taste good.

I went to Truth or Consequences a few years ago and saw my Uncle Monty Bussey. He told me I had missed seeing Proctor by two days as he had come by to see him. He doubted if Proctor remembered the visit since his mind was starting to wander. I saw in a Roswell paper some time later that one of his grandkids had gotten married to someone in Tyrone. He may still be living for I have not seen any notice otherwise.

Floyd and Loretta Proctor were on T.V. in September, 1989 on a prgram about U.F.O.s. Years ago, they had discovered burned extra-terrestrials on their property, but the army had come in and taken the bodies away and told them to keep quiet about it. The show aired again just recently, around the first week of October.

Book Review
by Arthur D. Martinez, Ph.D
Quijote City, U.S.A., Sybnication, Inc.
BATTLES AND LEADERS OF THE CIVIL WAR
Selected and Edited by Ned Bradford
Meridian Press; $10.95

I read this 620-page book while on vacation this past summer. Don't get me wrong; my family and I shared and enjoyed an exciting adventure in Belize, the Peten Region of Guatemala, and most of the Mexican Yucatan Peninsula. It was during the airport stopovers, the lengthy flights, the bus rides, and in the late evenings when the others were asleep that I would read **Battles and Leaders of the Civil War.**

I will admit that putting this book down was difficult for me to do. I always looked forward to picking it up again. Although I am not a Civil War buff, the era is familiar to me because of my general History and largely Political Science background. The U.S. Civil War has always held a deep, almost captivating interest for me. If I have a related bias, it is that I have always believed it was preferable and beneficial that the Union be preserved and that the slaves be freed.

From reading this book, one can come away amazed that the South actually lost the U.S. Civil War. Practically from the opening recollection to the final one, I received the impression that the Northern side was disorganized, militarily inept, bereft of capable leaders, and not at all a match for their Southern cousins on the battlefield.

Perhaps it was my bias, but it seemed to me that the selected articles gave a depiction -- whether intended or not -- of the South taking the initiative and keeping it throughout most of the Civil War. They were consistently victorious; seldom did they lose a battle; in fact, one gets the clear impression that they won practically every important battle, but lost the war. They lost, not because they were militarily inferior or less spirited, but because the North simply overwhelmed them with superior manpower, firepower, and economic power. One is led to believe that had the North not had these advantages, they could have lost the Civil War!

Reading page after page, recollection after recollection, I found myself almost longing for a Union victory, any victory. Finally, toward the latter one-third of the book, one is introduced to a gradual turnaround, with the North winning a few battles -- despite themselves.

This leads me to wonder whether there was a good, balanced selection of recollections taken from the original four volumes which were written by battlefield commanders and others some 20 years after the Civil War. I realize readers can and will differ on this point.

Another impression is that the Confederate leaders, i.e., military commanders, kept taking on a rather invincible, almost demigod, masters of the battlefield status; whereas, the reader is kept waiting, almost in vain, again through two-thirds of the 620-page compilation to discover any significant Union military brilliance. When a few Northern leaders finally do enter the military victory circle, they appear to succeed mostly due to the somewhat clumsy but constant application of superior force against the gallant South and its superior leaders.

A couple of memorable passages in the book -- from many, many First, there was the depiction of the soldiers, their individual bravery and their generally poor, humble background. For example, the Carolinian soldier "from the piney woods district," maimed from his battleground wounds suffered during the valiant though desperate defense of the Confederate capital at Richmond, Virginia who, when offered fancy delicacies by attending Southern upper class ladies, looks up innocently and gasps, "I ain't a-contradictin' you. It mout be good for me, but my stomick's kinder sot agin it. There ain't but one thing I'm sorter yarning arter, an that's a dish o' greens en bacon fat with a few molarses poured onto it."

This moving episode, as well as several others, revealed graphically that armies of soldiers do "travel on their stomachs" and, more than this, that battles are many times determined by whether the troopers received their bread, bacon, coffee or whatever. Time and again this reality emerges in Bradford's book. Tempers flared if rations were short or unavailable; and, conversely, morale and *esprit d'corps* were boosted to potential battlefield glory, once the commanders brought in the rations.

So I left my 16 year career and became a Xerox manager where I hired high school grad; this way I could finish what I started in the classroom. I learned there was more than one way to skin a cat, just like gramps said there was.

In between times, I met with presidents, generals, ambassadors, and captors while I worked in the prisoner of war issue for 12 years. You see, I loaned my husband to Vietnam and they kep him. I learned new meanings for rage, terror, and betrayal.

Now that brings us to 21 December, 1989 when I took a vacation in Pinos Altos in the Gila and felt shades of *deja vu*.

Someplace just before Cloudcroft, I began to feel emotions that I thought had been run over by bell curves, interrogation rooms, and the fast lane. I shut off the radio twice thinking I had heard drums. I could have sworn I heard the dancers knee bells in the wind. *But of course not.*

I smelled the smoke on the ceiling of the Cliff Dwellings and heard the village sounds, *but not really.* I touched the walls of the grainery *and found husk in my palm.* I shivered in the cold of the passing --- *breeze?*

No matter where I walked or drove in the Gila, I had the feeling of an escort. Even my dogs set to barking and going nuts for no apparent reason.

I met people whose eyes walked back into the old sacred Indian teachings and whose soul warmed mine with, of all things, *touch!*

I left, drowning my jacket with tears, feeling anger that I couldn't stay, frustrated that I didn't understand what I was feeling, resenting the spirits for stirring up my neatly ordered life, and knowing that I would not be whole again until I came back.

The people I met in P.A. introduced me to "family" in the Mimbres Valley. By the end of June, I was driving up the main Mimbres Valley Road and seeing vistas that made me say, "Yeah, I've seen that house before!" My throat was tight, the car's air conditioning wasn't cool enough, and it felt like my gas pedal had stopped working.

I could not concentrate on driving -- all I could do was take in each view almost foot by foot, yet collectively. By the time I got to the turnoff drive, I was captivated I felt overcome by the emotions of memory and of coming home.

When everyone poured out the door to greet me -- whom they had never met before -- I got hugged more in those first five minutes than I've been in my entire life.

By the time I'd taken three trips back, two monumental events had occurred.

In October, I attended the Community Concert event in Silver City that featured Irving Berlin music. We arrived early and I watched folks come in. Neighbor greeted neighbor, doctor/lawyer greeted client, student greeted teacher, mother greeted son and family, artist greeted customer, and I greeted the wafting waves of 50 years ago. I smiled away the tears in the lap of my original values.

That same visit, four acres of the valley spoke to me, and I spoke for it with earnest money. I sign the stewardship papers on 21 December 1990 -- exactly one year from my first walk back into time.

So, there you have it A story of coming and going, of learning and giving, of gigfiting andfeeling. If you'd like, I'll keep you up to date on my latest move antics, and the feeling of coming back home. If you like, I'll explore the stories that go with a paragraph that touched you in particular. If you like, I'll show you my poem, *The Sacred Side of Mimbres.*

In the meantime, may God and our Sacred Spirits warm you in his lap of Love and Light.

Cal & Nancy Thompson

106 West Broadway
Silver City, NM 88061-5093
(505) 388-1811

located in the historic district of downtown Silver City

TALES OF NEW MEXICO, TEXAS, AND ARIZONA

by Cecil G. Emery

Cecil Emery has lived in Grant County since 1930 except for brief spells in Arizona and Texas. He worked in the mines for 38 years. He also worked on various ranches in the area when the mines were down. It is on these ranches that he experienced all the colorful tales in his collection.

Meteorite in Fierro and Cyclones in Grant County

In November of 1932, I was working for McMillan Cattle Company. We were camped at the M---L Ranch south of Silver City and getting some cattle together.

About 4:00 a.m., a couple of men were wrangling horses east of the house and corrals. I was up on the hill west of the house, so I could hear the horses and men coming off the side of the hill.

All of a sudden a big roar started! A second or two later, the whole country turned as bright as day!... And then a huge explosion took place sort of in the direction of Santa Rita, but a little to the left of the pit. Right after the explosion, it lit up even bigger! I could see all the horses and men real plain.

The A.T. Cross remuda was about half white horses and half dark-colored horses so they were fairly easy to spot on dark nights or brightly moonlit nights. But this time they were all easy to see.

The first thing I thought of was the oil and gasoline storage tanks by the railroad tracks at Bayard Station (present day Bayard).

We found out two days later that it was a meteorite that had hit on the west side of the canyon by Fierro. A man living in Fierro who had a milk cow said she ran out but did not come in to be milked. When he got off work the next day, he went hunting for her and found her dead. All the hair was burned off her.

There was a good-sized patch of brush, he told me, that was burned and killed, and a hole. He said the earth was still warm. They dug a little

Cont'd →

→ Cont'd

and found some hard metal. He said it was 17 feet deep! They dug it out and brought it in to Silver City on the back bumper of the car. I believe it weighed 580 pounds.   They finally put it in Cosgrove Hardware's window on display for a while, and it finally disappeared.

A few days later, there was a report that an eight pound piece of the same meteorite was found close to Amarillo, Texas. It had set a grass fire. While they were fighting the fire they discovered the piece of metal. It was mostly made of nickel metal.

Cyclones are not very numerous in these parts, but they do happen. I have witnessed about three in person -- two in Arenas Valley and one just below Silver City.

The one below Silver City tore up one house close to the south side of Mr. Morton's golf course; then it went on towards Lone Mountain. I saw it dump a lot of ice. It was reported to have dumped some hails and slugs of ice in Central.

The two I saw in Arenas Valley near Whiskey Creek tore out the screens and the walls of the drive-in theatre at Whiskey Creek both times. The two cyclones I saw happened just 30 days apart. The first one tore out a huge cottonwood tree at the old race track property. The tree stood about ten feet from the corner of the old adobe house, but it only tore about two feet off the corner of the house. That house had been there many years. I never saw any damage report, but there were not many houses around at that time.

Close to the head of Pack Saddle Canyon, just west of Goose Lake, there is a pretty good stand of timber. The trail goes through it to go on into the canyon.

One time when Clyde Wootan and I were on this trail, we got to the timber and discovered there was no trail left! All we saw was a swath about 400 feet wide in which all the timber was just twisted and tangled. We had to make another trail to get off into the canyon. There was no evidence that anyone else had been there since this wreck had taken place.

In 1934 I saw the same kind of a mess at Snow Park on the east side of Mogollon Baldy. The Forest Service had to use dynamite and cross cut saws to make a trail through to go to Baldy. The timber was so twisted you could not even walk through it. It was not just a big blowdown which happens regularly in thick timber, especially when the ground is really saturated and a big, straight, hard wind picks up -- no, it was a cyclone.

coming to his store from all over. Hoping to see them race for their free turkey certificates, he was disappointed to find out that many animal activists are vegetarians.

However, he was quite pleased Saturday morning when about 100 poor people in need of Thanksgiving turkeys showed up.

To make a bad joke worse, the Cessna dropped the majority of the certificates on private property, so many poor people went away disappointed.   Be sure to catch pictures of the gala event in the forthcoming issue of The Mustang.

Happy "Funny" Thanksgiving from. KNFT in Silver City and Farmers Supermarket in Deming.

The idea of a turkey throw is not even original. A few years ago, the TV sit-com WKRP which was based on a Cincinnati radio station featured a story with this same stunt. The "humor" was that they went through with it never realizing that turkeys can't fly. It didn't seem funny then, either.

However, if the personnel at KNFT feel driven to torment the humane people in our society, they should at least come up with an idea of their own.

THE HUNTING TRADITION: A BLIGHT UPON WILDLIFE AND HUMANITY

On November 7, a 32 year old family man was murdered at point blank range by an arrogant hunter who was illegally spotlighting deer [shining a bright light into the trees and blinding a deer into a stand-still target]. Both spotlighting and hunting on private land are against the law.   Freeman Lee Davis of Lindrith, NM was sitting in the cab of his truck as he and his wife attempted to steer the hunters away from his property by telling them spotlighting was illegal when when they pointed a gun in the window of Davis' truck and murdered him.

The Lindrith community complains about hunters every year but law enforcement officials say they don't have enough manpower to control the problem. Even though the Lindrith area is about 90% private land, the hunters swoop down on the community every year with about ten hunters to every deer.

In Bangor, Maine, a jury freed a hunter who killed a 37 year old mother of twin one year old girls. Karen Wood had been standing just 130 feet behind her home when the hunter mistook her white mittens for the underside of a deer. *The El Paso Times* states that "some people even suggested that Karen Wood was at fault for wearing the mittens during hunting season. They hinted that because she was 'from away' -- a term used to describe people from other states - she was ignorant of Maine's hunting tradition." Last year, 216,476 people bought hunting licenses in Maine and killed 30,260 deer.

Perhaps the following book review will shed light on the fact that some traditions are primitive and need to be discontinued; otherwise, all our wildlife will be killed off and many more human beings will be needlessly killed in the process.

DEMOLISHING THE RATIONALIZATIONS

A Book Review by Laura Moretti

The American Hunting Myth

by Ron Baker

Vantage Press, 1985, 287 pages; $10.95 cloth

Every day *more than half a million* wild animals are killed in the U.S. as a result of the ministrations of recreational hunters, ranchers, farmers, and zealous "wildlife managers" and trappers.

That these crude and barbaric activies should take place in the age of computers, trips to the moon and heart transplants is a baffling commentary on the contradictions of culture and the staying power of brutality disguised as hallowed tradition. More often than not, the animals succumb to an awesome array of weapons and artifacts concocted by the human mind, ranging from all sorts of specialized ammunition, legholds, snares, spears, arrows, and traps to diabiolical poisons, electrification, and even aerial hunts. The inevitable result of so much malignant enterprise is the maiming, rippling and disrupting of living nature to a degree unthinkable in more technologically primitive times.

Ironically, the hunters and the government bureaucrats who work hand-in-glove with them insist on caling these depraved activities "conservation," "wildlife management," and other innocuous-sounding terms in the hope of dulling the public's perception of what really goes on.

For the most part the propaganda works. But now Ron Baker, a noted ecologist who has his facts as straight as his sense of ethics, has taken the trouble to codify in a systematic way the myriad self-serving rationalizations, arguments, and pretensions advanced by the hunting lobby, and produced a book that may singlehandedly demolish much of this edifice of lies.

Not since Cleveland Amory's 1974 book, **Man Kind? Our Incredible War on Wildlife**, has a text such a thoroughness been written about the disastrous practice of "recreational" hunting. But what Amory's book did to the image of American "sport hunters," Ron Baker's **The American Hunting Myth** does to the entire system of wildlife management.

Several excellent books about sport hunting have been written (Lewis Regenstein's **The Politics of Extinction** comes to mind, for example), but their impact, both on the animal rights movement and the general public has remained limited. Amory's book was a shocking expose that thrust hunting and the whole fraternity of miscreants into the line of fire; but when the numbers were tallied and the priorities picked, factory

TALES OF NEW MEXICO, TEXAS, AND ARIZONA

by Cecil G. Emery

Cecil Emery has lived in Grant County since 1930 except for brief spells in Arizona and Texas. He worked in the mines for 38 years. He also worked on various ranches in the area when the mines were down. It is on these ranches that he experienced all the colorful tales in his collection.

Cruz Smith: 1937 to 1942

Cruz Smith was quite old and lived in the Lower Cooney Place on the Mimbres River. The old shack had only pieces of roof, but it kept dry in spots. It had an old stove with part of the legs missing so rocks were put under it to level it up. There was an old table and a homemade cupboard with some shelves.

About a half or three-fourths of a mile above Cruz Smith's shack on the Lower Cooney was another log house that was a Cooney Place, too. Across from it was the grave of one Cooney who was shot to death in a chair leaned back against the side of the building.

There were two 30/30 shells in the thicket across from where the grave is. They claimed they never found out who killed Cooney.

After one Cooney died, the other one left and the Cooney places bleonged to the G. O. S. Cattle Company shortly after.

Cruz Smith told me he was German and Mexican; he could speak Spanish very well. He told me he had been married and had a daughter in Deming.

He was very interesting to talk to and he certainly knew his part of the country. I really do not know just how much country that included.

Ben Endlich told me that he and Cruz Smith were both hired as bodyguards to Vic Culberson.

Cruz could shoot the eye out of a squirrel in a tall pine tree and did so in my presence when he was in his 70s. He could also get a turkey when he needed to.

One game warden tricked him into showing him how to get a turkey; he didn't tell him he was a game warden until he arrested him. Well, he had no money, so they turned him out; but he never would show any one else how to get any game.

Cruz would always offer you something to drink or eat, but the dishes were always dirty. He would let his hair grow real long. Now and then he would cut it, tie it together, and hang the tied-up hair on the edge of the dish cupboard -- Wasn't anything very appetizing!

One time when I moved camp I gave Cruz a good-sized piece of fresh beef -- a hind quarter. About a week later, I came by the Cooney place and he had it hanging on the eave of the house. It had got sort of putrid and had fly blows and maggots. When he saw me look at it, he said he was ripening it so it would be good.

When I came by another time, he had a turkey hanging the same way and it was in the same shape, but he had not gutted it. It was very blue. Very ripe.

In the early 1940s, Cruz Smith was found in a big drift down on the Mimbres River below the Cooney place, dead after a good-sized flood. He had been dead several days, the authorities stated.

Somewhere in the Rockies, on a warm outcropping, mother puma is being mauled by her spotted young, her whiskers pulled and ears nipped as she gently pushes them back. She lays curled but flowing, like a golden-furred lake bordered by sandstone. When she moves, she embodies the physics of water, weighty liquid waves, one ripple after another beneath loose-hung skin. Always flowing.

She doesn't jump down the rocks, but cascades over them, hindquarters and tufted tail following the front half through some invisible river channel. She flows down the dry wash, the *arroyo seco*, and blends into the mountain's seeps and fissures.

To protect the lion is to guard a secret too special for the telling, save a spirit floating noiselessly somewhere outside the limits of your experience. It means protecting a poetic ensemble of fur and claw, a set of somber yellow orbs staring out of the Pleistocene towards an uncertain

future. They are the feel of water in the shape of a cat, an artistic subject of the greatest beauty, a vision of grace you will proabably never lay eyes on... Art you may never see... Music you may never hear. With puma, we learn the medicine of appreciating *that which is not there for us.*

A man looks into a pool of water. He sees a reflection of himself and, apart from that, he sees a reflection of the world.

A lion looks into a pool of water, and sees the world.

Author's Note:

Since these magnificent animals can only be killed with dogs or traps, demanding the permanent ban of both methods is the surest legal solution. Write the Department of Game and Fish, Santa Fe, NM 87501 and your representatives.

A hearing on lions in Silver City was heavily in support of their protection here, in the wildest of the Southwestern ranges. Thank you!

TALES OF NEW MEXICO, TEXAS, AND ARIZONA
by Cecil G. Emery

Cecil Emery has lived in Grant County since 1930 except for brief spells in Arizona and Texas. He worked in the mines for 38 years. He also worked on various ranches in the area when the mines were down. It is on these ranches that he experienced all the colorful tales in his collection.

BILL WATSON AND
THE CAMP ROBBER
-- 1936 --

My wife Ruth's brother, Bill Watson, was living in Mogollon with his family when the Fannie Mine shut down. He took a wood-cutting job close to Willow Creek. Everybody was broke then so you just made do with whatever you had.

Bill made his camp as close to a small spring of water as he could. He found a big tree for shade and as a place to hang what groceries he had so the varmints wouldn't ruin his chuck.

He had a good-sized woodpile close by camp. His bed was under the tree to shield against any possible rain since he did not have a tent and not even a very good bed tarp.

Bill was a good worker and he worked as long as he could see each day. He was getting paid by the cord to cut the wood, but it was only a dollar and a half per cord. He fed himself, but pickin's was sort of slim.

By night he would be dead tired and he would almost die when he hit the sack.

Along in the middle of the night something woke him up when it stepped on him! When he came awake, the moon was shining on the outline of a *good-sized bear!* This giant bear was *standing* on Bill, reaching up after the groceries tied up in the tree!

Bill got loose from his bed and took off barefooted in his drawers. The bear continued to get the bacon and flour and everything Bill had. He ate what he liked and tore up the rest while Bill shivered up a sweat in his birthday suit up on the hillside. The only weapons Bill had were his ax and some rocks, and his ax was on the woodpile, so he was stranded there all night.

Along after sunup, some boys from the Willow Creek Three C camp came up looking for their pet bear that had run off from camp.

When they found Bill and the bear they teased Bill for a while but later took him down to camp and replaced some groceries and bedding that the bear had destroyed.

Bill said he still could not tell that he was a tame bear even after daylight. He said that he never did feel too easy camping there by himself after that incident.

I wish I could have seen Bill race away from that bear, for Bill could really run even *without* thinking that a bear was after him!

Gwynne opened the Gila Valley Health Center in August, 1989 and presently maintains a private practice there in massage therapy while continuing her studies toward a naturopathic doctor certification. The Health Center is located at 3 Clark Road in Gila and the number there is 1-535-2400.

Gwynne is now also offering two continuing education classes at WNMU in which she will teach the healing art of massage therapy. Massage Therapy 1 will be offered on Monday nights from 6 - 9 from March 4 - April 22 -- a total of 8 weeks. The class will focus on techniques for effective massage such as hand positions, strokes, massage sequence, indications, and contraindications for massage; also included will be studies in basic anatomy, body awareness, and reflexology. Students will ultimately learn to create their own massage movements.

Massage Therapy 2 classes will meet on Saturdays from 11 - 4 from March 9 - April 6 -- a total of five weeks. In this class, students will study trigger point therapy, therapeutic stretches for muscular release, intuitive massage, reflexology, body reading, and related healing arts.

THIS ONE, AGAIN
by Katrina

I know the past is yesterday.
 I know that's not HIS grave.
 I know the Taps are echoes,
  above some other "Brave."

But all "I know" gets lost in tears,
  beside a flag-draped coffin.
While watching prisoners on parade,
  the past sneaks up too often!

For war is war -- all nations bleed.
 It's hard to watch the news.
We want to know, but please don't show,
 a face that we might lose.

Reservists now are warriors.
 Old foes now sit beside.
The answers throw up questions,
 while bombs and bones collide.

  Can Courage marry Sanity?
  Can tears cause Fire to Cease?
 Can greed and hate die of neglect?
  CAN YOU FIND MISSING PEACE?

-- This poem speaks to the memories of yesterday that are stirred in with the smells and sounds of today. It speaks to the wish for settling things another way and the disappointment that that way is not looked for honestly enough before the trigger is pulled. It speaks to the soul of me that grieves for all of all nations -- for the missing piece is truly PEACE!

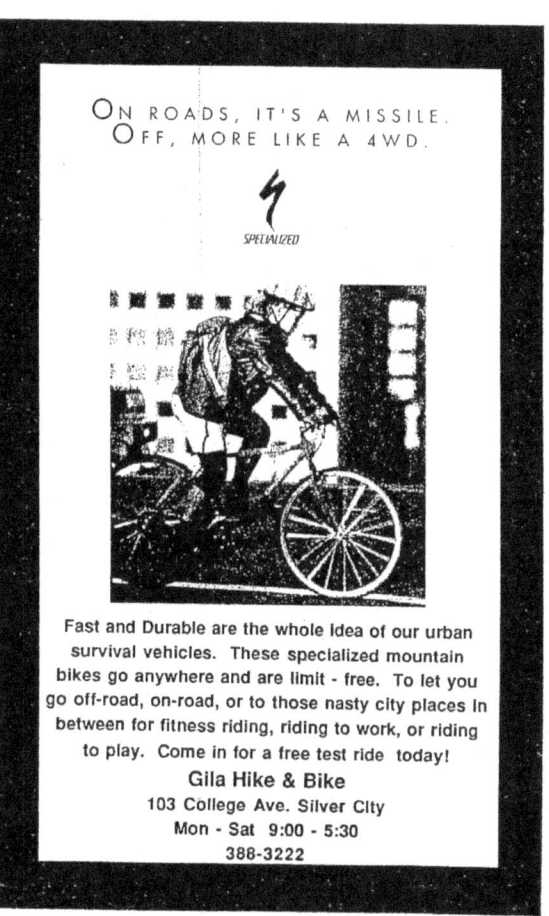

TALES OF NEW MEXICO, TEXAS, AND ARIZONA

by Cecil G. Emery

Cecil Emery has lived in Grant County since 1930 except for brief spells in Arizona and Texas. He worked in the mines for 38 years. He also worked on various ranches in the area when the mines were down. It is on these ranches that he experienced all the colorful tales in his collection.

FRANK AND ADA SCHULTZ 1936 to 1987

In 1936 we were living in Central Heights, Arizona. Ruth's dad was running a grocery and gas station there. Frank Schultz came there and rented a cabin. He stayed around the store some and he would prowl the nearby towns of Globe and Claypool and Miami, but he would always come back to talking to John Watson and watching the trade. Finally, he and John made a trade and Frank bought the store from him.

Frank married soon after that. His wife was named Ada and they lived in the back of the store and ran it. We were living close by so we traded some with Frank. When our first son, Jim, was born there in July of 1936, they both took up with him and would keep him if we went someplace now and then. They both had been married before, we found out, ad both had children, but we never knew any of them.

When my job played out in October of 1937, we left Arizona and came back to Grant County. When we left, we did not have much money, so Frank insisted that we fill up with gas and oil and take some extra oil and some groceries on credit till I got a job. Well, I was lucky enough to go to work two days after we arrived, so we were able to pay them back and let them know where we were located. We stayed in touch the rest of our lives; they were our friends down through the years.

Frank loved to tell me stories about things that he had done and places he had been. He was born in Kansas in 1897 and raised there near Kansas City. He joined the army at age 17 and when Pershing was sent to Old Mexico after Pancho Villa raided Columbus in 1916, he was the head mechanic. They had one plane at first, and a little later on they had two planes. Pershing had Frank go with him everywhere as his pilot and mechanic during the time they were trying to pursue Pancho.

Frank liked flying and went to Europe in Worl War I as a pilot. After the war was over, he stayed in the army for some years and got married for a short time, but his kids stayed with their mother. I saw some pictures of his kids ands one or two of Ada's kids also, mostly after they were grown.

About one year after we left Central Heights, they moved to Wickenburg, Arizona and started prospecting. He also got some goats and had some pasture land. He developed some gold and silver claims and did some dry washing in the washes where he lived. He found some colors and thousands of arrowheads and bone and turquoise beads, and some turquoise chunks.

One day he dug up a large egg-shaped rock and started to toss it to one side, but then he took a second look; he took his knife blade and scraped it and behold, it was turquoise! When he cleaned it up, it weighed 17 pounds! It was eight inches across the big end and tapered to about two inches at the small end. He kept it for a lot of years before it was cut.

Along about 1940, they moved to Phoenix and Ada worked as a nurse's aid. Frank went to work at an aviation firm in the Phoenix area as an instructor.

When World War II came up, he trained pilots for the U.S. Right around then, he and Ada came to see us and stayed a few days. He went prospecting, of course, on Bear Creek north of Pinos Altos and got a few colors in several locations. Sometimes we went with him and prowled in some of the old workings. It was just an outing for us, but he was quite serious.

At that time, I was working in the Asarco Mine at Vanadium. While I was at work, an incident took place at our home that was not really funny at the time but, as time went by, it got funny.

While Frank was in the outhouse one hot day, our son, Jim, slipped out and tied the door shut and would not come back and let him out. Finally, Ruth and Ada heard the commotion and got things under control. Ada thought it was funny at the time, but did not dare let on to Frank that she thought it was funny. For awhile, Jim was not Frank's favorite, but years later he could laugh about it, too.

They went back to Phoenix after that visit and Frank went on training men who were being shipped out for overseas duty. After the third bunch of trainees had been shipped, he told the head officers he would go AWOL if he was not sent, too. They shipped him overseas and he flew a lot of missions over Europe. But then they sent him to North Africa and he finally got shot down and busted up so bad he was sent to a hospital in Florida.

Ada was working in Phoenix and having a time of it making ends meet; of course, she was also doing a lot of worrying. After about a year, Frank told the army he wanted to go back. He told them he could make it again. They sent him to the South Pacific, but they would not let him fly. He was a maintenance officer for the best of the war. After he came home, they visited with us for a few days and then headed out for Phoenix.

After about a week went by, we got a letter from them out of Lordsburg. They had stopped at the nine mile station west of Lorsdburg and the Duncan Highway to eat a bit and just bought the place. It was a little store with one gas pump and a hamburger stand. They had to haul water from Lordsburg as they had no well.

They were in the middle of 80 acres of state land; the highway split it with about 20 acres on the north side and the rest of the land was south of the road. It was joining Sherwood Culberson's ranch so Frank bought the land and leased a gravel pit to the highway for road work. He later leased the grazing to Sherwood and eventually sold it to him.

On the land on the north side he planted pecan trees and built three or four cabins. He did tune-up jobs as well as some mechanic jobs. Ada put out a lot of good meals as well as some hamburgers. Frank had a lapidary shop and always had some gem rocks to sell and trade. He finally bought a well rig and drilled a deep well, but he never got much water so he continued to haul some water. He would buy things to sell and go to sheriff's sales. They were doing all right and gradually making a real go of the place.

But when the state and government decided to widen the road, they chose to widen it by the side where their business was and all the other buildings as well. Frank would not sell for the price they fixed when they condemned it, so one day when they returned from Lorsdburg they found locks on everything. The law would not let them in except to get their personal things. They had to take what was offered for the buildings and stock in the store. Everything was cleared off. He finally sold the remaining 12 acres several years after they moved back to Phoenix. It is still vacant, or was the last time I went by the place.

Frank wrote me that he had sold part of the 17 pound turquoise chunk. He said the price of turquoise was very high so if I could get him some here at the mines, he would give me as much as $30 a pound. I had to tell him that turquoise was $200 a pound here and very scarce.

When I went to Phoenix a short time later, I found out that he had sold eight pounds of the big end of the stone for $900. The shop he sold to sliced the remaining 9 pounds up for him real well. Frank was a good

Cont'd →

→ Cont'd

silversmith so he used the turquoise to make belt buckles, bolos, pendants, pens, bracelets, and earrings. He got a nice price out of all of his jewelry, but he never got any more turquoise equal to the piece he had sold, nor as good, for the big stone was flawless.

After Frank came home from World War II and the war started in Korea, he said he believed he would bow out and let someone else do the fighting for awhile.

Frank remained as straight as a poker all his life, but he finally got Alzheimer's disease and he had to be put in a rest home. When we went to see Ada and Frank, she had a trailer home and went every day to feed him at least one good meal as he was too blind to see his food. He knew us for a few seconds, then went off into the blue yonder.   When he passed away, I believe he was 87 years old.

Ruth and I and our sons would hear from Ada occasionally until about 1987 when one of Ada's nieces answered our letter and said that Ada had passed away a short time ago.   Ada was also straight all her life and to us she was a wonderful person.

Frank was a very honest man all his life and a true friend. I enjoyed hearing the stories of his life. He never bragged, he just told it like he thought it really was.

A GOOD THOUGHT FOR ANY DAY
by Alma Hollis

Whosoever believes in Him should not perish but have everlasting life.
John 3:16

A happy, happy birthday one and all
Whether you are short or tall.
Do you worry about getting old?
Well, this is what I've been told.
My Sunday school teacher said,
"You'd better be glad,
        you could be dead!"
So thank God for His wonderful gift
Trusting in Him will give you a lift
As long as you have life
He will help you with all strife.

IS A BURGER WORTH IT?
Reprinted from the **Vegetarian Times**

You may already know that America's meat-based diet is the perpetrator of all sorts of environmental ills. Still, it's often difficult to imagine how much of an impact switching to a vegetarian diet can have in alleviating some of that stress on the planet. Here are some eye-opening statistics to help you grasp the connection.

** Estimated rate of worldwide tropical rainforest deforestation per minute: 150 acres; per day: 216,000 acres.

** Percentage of tropical rainforest deforestation directly linked with livestock raising: more than 50%.

** Amount of forest lost for every hamburger produced from livestock raised on what was Central American forest: 55 square feet.

** Current rate of species extinction due to destruction of tropical rainforests and related habitats: 1,000 per year

** Year in which Central and South America will be stripped of tropical rainforest if present rate of deforestation continues: 2010

** How often an acre of U.S. trees disappears: every 8 seconds

** Number of acres of U.S. forest used for grazing or growing feed for livestock for every acre cleared for urban development: 7 acres.

** Amount of trees spared per year by each individual who switches to a vegan diet: 1 acre

** Water needed to produce one pound of wheat: 25 gallons. Water needed to produce one pound of meat: 2,500 gallons.

** Amount of water conserved each year by switching to a lacto-vegetarian diet: 1,095,000 gallons (1 1/2 Olympic-sized pools).

** Amount of U.S. topsoil lost to date: about 2/3.

** Percentage of U.S. topsoil loss due to livestock raising: at least 85%

** Percentage of U.S. agricultural land used for livestock production (including pasture, rangeland, and cropland): 87%.

** Percentage of total U.S. land used for livestock: 45%

** Average amount of meat eaten by each American annually: 190 pounds.

** Number of people who could be adequately fed by the grain saved if Americans reduced their intake of meat by 10%: 60 million people.

** Percentage of Americans who call themselves environmentalists: 76%.

** Percentage of Americans who are vegetarian: 2.8%

TALES OF NEW MEXICO, TEXAS, AND ARIZONA
by Cecil G. Emery

Cecil Emery has lived in Grant County since 1930 except for brief spells in Arizona and Texas. He worked in the mines for 38 years. He also worked on various ranches in the area when the mines were down. It is on these ranches that he experienced all the colorful tales in his collection.

JACK RUTLAND

I met Jack Rutland in the summer of 1931. He was close to 80 years old then but in 1932 I was around him almost daily. He was an old bachelor who had come to America as a very young man from England -- a cousin Jack.

In 1932 he was sort of doddery -- his voice was quavery and his eyes watered all the time, but he could read and never wore glasses. He had a perpetual dip of snuff except at meal time and bed time. The amber would forever be ready to drip off his long mustache. He could talk Spanish fluently and a little Apache, too.

Jack and I did quite a few jobs together and a few times when harnesses, saddles, and other material disappeared, he could find them. He would say just take me to some certain location and he would always be right about who was responsible for taking the objects, and we would recover them. Sometimes we would find property buried, and once I saw a man whip three of his sons that were as old as 20 when it was discovered that they had taken some of our harnesses. They brought all the harnesses back to us.

At night when we were not working, we would meet at someone's room in the bunkhouse at the Gila Farms or the old L.C. Farm headquarters. It was there a few people told me of Jack being a wagon cook and he told me a few tales about things that took place. He did not claim to have been a cowboy but he knew a bit about horses.

Jack told a story about one man I knew who had come to the L.C. wagon at mid-morning and wanted to see Tom Johnson, the wagon boss. Jack told him that he had been given orders to have dinner ready when they got in with the cattle to work -- about noon to 1 p.m. Jack started to make bread and he was working the dough when he noticed he was being watched by this man. Jack asked him if he was going to stay around for dinner. He told Jack it depended on which way the drip fell; he was watching the snuff amber hanging on the end of Jack's mustache.

Jack told me about working for the Swann Cattle Company down by Lordsburg. Mr. Swann died and left a wife and some daughters but no sons. Jack had been their foreman so Mrs. Swann told the girls they had to get his consent to do whatever came along, just like they had their father. Jack said it was the time when people were bicycle crazy over bicycles that had big wheels in front and small wheels at the back. One of the girl's beaux wanted to give her a bicycle so she asked Jack if it would be all right. He told her after studying a while that he did not think it would be right for any of the girls to take anything between their legs that would not stand alone.

Mrs. Swann and one daughter who was a Dr. Moss's wife came to see Jack one day and stayed all day at the Gila Farms visiting with him. He introduced me to them and I learned that they lived in Clifton, Arizona at the time. Jack said he had spent most of his life working for the Swanns and the L.C. outfit.

Jack and I were witnesses for a trial that took place in Silver City. Jack was looking out a window through a screen and when the shooting took place he got a little blood and a piece of flesh from a gunshot wound in his mustache and some in one eye. The trial was an all day affair. I was on the witness stand first and then some more. Jack came last, and when his testimony was over, he was excused. At that point, he went up to Judge Dunifonand and shook hands with him. Then he said, "Judge, are you through with Cecil and I?"

"Yes," the judge.

"Well," said Jack, "I've got a 150 hogs to feed and I need to get home and get at it, and Cecil is my chauffeur."

The Judge said, "You can go feed your hogs."

In 1932 when I was working with Jack and I was trucking some, I got acquainted with Walter Moore on the Mimbres River. I told him that Jack Rutland had told me to talk to him as they were old acquaintances. Walter told me that he came from Kentucky to the Mimbres Valley in 1878 when he was nine years old. All the people who came with him were in wagons with ox teams except Jack, a young man from England who led them to the Mimbres on a horse.

In 1938 I talked to Walter Moore again when I was working for the G.O.S. Ranch. He said that in 1878 when he and Jack arrived, the old Moore Ranch was known as the Ace Christmas Ranch. In 1938 they were taking the picket fence posts out and turning them over because they were rotting off at the bottom. Walter said they were put in the corral in 1878 when they first came there.

Jack, who still rode a good, old, gentle horse, told me that he had not been paid his wages for two years and that he had loaned Mr. Julian Bassett $2800 cash and had never been repaid. They had agreed to deed him a small piece of farmland if they could not get the cash to pay him. It was to be just north of George Clark's home across the road from George's house.

There were 35 of us working there that could not get any money so I was designated to see a lawyer in Silver City about collecting our wages. Jack had the most coming to him of anyone.

Four lawyers in Silver City advised me to go to the courthouse and look up any livestock property owned by Basset and try to trade him out of anything that was not mortgaged. They said that even though the state law said you could not be beat out of lawful wages, that no one would undertake going to court against Julian Basset who was representing himself. I reported back and six of us just traded out with Mr. Bassett for some cattle and horses and mules. But 29 took the case to court and they lost. Jack never got anything ever; he kept working, hoping to get his money, but he never did. Mr. Wooley, the bookkeeper, told me personally that he got all his wages because if any money came in he got his first.

After Bassett lost all his holdings in New Mexico and went back to Dryden, Texas Jack had no money and got to where he could not work, so George Clark and his sons George Jr. and Claude built an adobe bunkhouse for Jack. It was close to where George and Jack and George Jr. lived so he would eat with the family. George Jr. and Jack had a spit and whittle club since Jack dipped snuff and George was practicing chewing plug tobacco.

While George Clark was working for the Forest Service with me in 1934, George got word that Jack had died. He went to Gila to bury Jack Rutland and he had to foot the bill for the funeral. Jack had been euchred out of what little he had managed to save all his life.

There are probably very few people left today who remember Jack Rutland.

TALES OF NEW MEXICO, TEXAS, AND ARIZONA
by Cecil G. Emery

Angel Bustos in 1940

Angel Bustos worked with me for a while at the Asarco Groundhog Mine. He also worked at the Inspiration Mine in Miami, Arizona as an engineer on the underground railroad where his brother was killed while working with Angel on a train. Angel was a small man and only had one eardrum left.

He told me about some of his early life. His father worked out at the Merchom Mine on Salt Creek on the north side of the Sapillo (Sapillo Creek is approximately 40 miles from Silver City). His folks all lived at the mine so when school was in session Angel stayed with a man and woman who were both school teachers (and both gringos) in Silver City. He was nine years old at the time. Aside from going to school, there were a few things he was told to do each week. One was to keep the shoes of the household all polished up, especially the man's shoes.

One day in October he was playing and did not do what he was supposed to do. He said the man never got cranky with him, but he was afraid he would catch heck so he took some money out of his weekly allowance, bought a big sack of candy, and took off from Silver City toward Pinos Altos. By the time he got to Pinos Altos, he had eaten quite a bit of the candy, but then he ran into some boys and they took the rest of it away from him. "I was pretty mad," he said, "but they were bigger and there were more of them."

He headed on to Cherry Creek and out by Meadow Creek (that was the only road in those days). When he got to Meadow Creek, he was very thirsty so he knelt down to drink. As he leaned over to drink, he noticed some big bear tracks in the sand and suddenly he wasn't thirsty anymore. He just took off toward the Sapillo in a hurry. He knew they were bear tracks because his uncle had taken him hunting the year before and had shown him bear tracks so he recognized them pretty quickly.

The old road went off into Hill Canyon on the Sapillo above the Biddle place about opposite railroad Canyon's mouth. Angel traveled down the Sapillo to the old Goforth place and up Salt Creek two or thee miles to the Merchom Mine; luckily, he got there before sundown. When he got to the mine his dad and mother wanted to know what had happened. When he told them, they hooked up a team and started back toward town. That night, about half way there, they met up with the school teacher coming out to the Sapillo. He had gotten a team and trailed Angel.

"I didn't get a whipping," he said, "but I should have... I never gave them any more trouble. They were like family to me all my life. They saw that I got some education. The schoolteacher and my father were real good friends."

The old road Angel traveled was used way back in the old days so it still had ox shoes along it. There was an old ox yoke in the fork of a big juniper tree between Meadow Creek and the Ridge going off to the mouth of Hill Canyon. I heard that Hub Estes sent a man to get the ox yoke with a pack mule. The tree had grown around the yoke in the fork so it probably took quite a lot of work to get it out.

ANIMAL LIBERATION
by Bob Young

Kate has kindly consented to give me a regular column on "animal rights." I will replace that term for "animal liberation" since it has become questionable as to whether nonhuman animals can have "rights" in the sense that we have invented them for ourselves. Actually, the question is moot since we are also animals... primates, as a matter of biological fact.

These articles will be about the tyranny of human animals over nonhuman animals. Our beloved America has become the most" animal-inhumane society" in the history of human civilization. We have used modern technology to turn BILLIONS of nonhuman animals into research tools, food production units, and bogus wildlife management victims.

Humans have been abusing other animals since the dawn of history. Their suffering today is largely the inheritance of millenia of culturally conditioned human-centered prejudice. In the Western World, particularly, nonhuman animals have traditionally been regarded as little more than "things" to be exploited for pleasure and profit, with minor concern for their well-being.

In the Judaeo-Christian tradition, the exploitation of animals begins with Genesis. In the Garden of Eden, humans' "dominion over the earth" did not include the killing of animals for food. The "parents" of the human race were vegetarians. But after the Fall, the slaughter began.

To Noah, God said: "The fear of you and the dread of you shall be upon every beast of the earth, and upon every fowl of the air, upon all that moveth upon the earth, and upon the fishes of the sea; into your hands they are delivered. Everything that liveth shall be meat for you." (Genesis 9: 1 - 3).

This ancient myth provided the rationalization for the grotesque practice of eating other animals.

Genesis set the tone for Western civilization. It only remained for Rene Descarte, the 17th century French philosopher, to augment this exploitative doctrine with the bizarre notion that nonhuman animals are mere machines, incapable of feeling or thought.

This philosophy of exploitation gave Western humanity its *carte blanche* to launch conscience-free into the destruction of the natural world order.

The fearful people who wrote the Bible probably never imagined that they were presenting the blueprint for global disaster.

(Next time... The origins of the modern animal liberation movement.)

TALES OF NEW MEXICO, TEXAS, AND ARIZONA
by Cecil G. Emery

B.D. HUGHES: BACHELOR RANCHER AND FARMER

Mr. B.D. Hughes came to the plains of Texas in the early 1900s. He bought up more and more till he had a nice little ranch. He dry farmed a little but mostly raised cattle.

B.D. Hughes nearly always had some young couple who were just trying to get started working for him on the shares. He would furnish everything, and the wife would cook and keep house. There would be a small money wage each month, and when the crops and cattle were sold they would get a percentage.

Most of the couples I knew would be able to get out on their own in a few years. If they needed a good word put in for them with some merchant, he would help them by telling the merchant that they were good, steady people.

Oscar Bibby was one man I knew who got his start that way. He and his wife were neighbors of ours for several years and we did business with them.

We bought cattle for several years from B.D.Hughes. He was close and dependable for whatever he said he would do. A Mr. Piggot, a Jewish cattle buyer, sometimes did business with Mr. Hughes, too. He called him Mr. P.D.Q's. We asked him who he meant and he said, "Well, most people called him B.D. Hughes. But he's always telling people that he's going to be doing something 'pretty damn quick,' so I just call him P.D. Q."

Sometimes we would get a bunch of cattle together and get ready to ship. Piggot would come along and buy everything to take to the feed pens so we would be saved the risk of shipping. Sometimes we could not trade, but it worked out most of the time.

Mr. Hughes was sometimes good for a little amusement. There were a few old maids and old widow women, and sometimes men would see this as an opportunity to have a little fun.

One widow woman was Mrs. Janes. She had a small farm and ranch which she was running by herself. She was having trouble with one of her bullslls not being able to breed cows right, so she asked a store man (Vince Stambaugh, who also had cattle) what to do.

Vince saw B.D. Hughes up the street, so he and two more men told her that B.D. Hughes knew more about things like that than they did. So she went out in the street and tied into Mr. Hughes.

I went along behind, just a few feet away, to see what would happen when Mrs. Janes spoke to him. When B.D. Hughes looked down the street, he spotted Vince and the other men watching from the doorway. He knew, then, that something was up. So when Mrs. Janes asked him a question about the bull's performance, he just told her this:

"Well," he said, " get a brick and tie a stiff wire on it with a hook on the end of the wire. Then, when the bull mounts the cow, hang the wire on his tool. That will hold it down to where it will fit." After saying that, B.D. Hughes just turned around and walked off.

"Thank you, I'll try that," Mrs. Janes called after him.

When it was over, the old man just looked at me and winked. I was 15 years old and we had known each other for at least ten years of my life at that time.

Not a one of the men ever mentioned to Mr. B.D. Hughes anything about the incident.

When I was 17 years old, I was working for Vince Stambaugh breaking wheat land and some raw land, too. Mr. B.D. Hughes was a good friend so he usually stopped by the place where I was working when he was going or coming to town to visit with the Stambaugh's. When he did not show up for a longer time than usual, we got a little concerned. Finally, he showed up looking pretty well bunged up. We finally got him to tell us what happened.

A couple who had come there (another trade deal) some three months before had tied him up and tortured him till he had finally given them a check for $1500! He had more money in the bank, but the people knew that someone would be suspicious if they tried for too much. He said the man and woman who did this to him thought he had money hidden around the place. He had had a hard time convincing them he did not have any money hidden in his home.

After they got the money, they just left him tied up. It took him two days to work loose.

They were never apprehended that I ever heard of.

Mr. B.D. Hughes was very wary of who he hired after that incident. He was sort of afraid to be with anyone he did not know, but he was good to everyone he thought was a friend. Up until that incident, he had thought everyone was his friend.

▄▄▄▄▄▄▄▄▄▄▄▄▄▄▄▄▄▄▄▄▄▄▄▄

DREAMS
by Deborah White

Relax.
In chasing your dreams they only run further and faster away.
So quit chasing them!
Sit quietly and listen.
Like a wild, frightened kitten,
your dreams scamper up the highest tree,
onto a limb
just out of your reach.
It knows your desperation, anger, and frustration
and in turn feels it must hide.
Relax.
Never give up on your dream.
Keep the dream alive in your heart.
Never forget the tiny cat,
but don't yell at it to come to you.
Relax.
Sit quietly and listen.
Let it come and sit beside you.
Let it get used to your smell.
Talk to it softly.
Tell it how glad you are that it is here.
How lucky you are to have it with you.
Let the kitten -- Your Dream --
come to you and nestle against you.
Together the two of you will purr with satisfaction.
Let the dream come to you and come true.

TALES OF NEW MEXICO, TEXAS, AND ARIZONA
by Cecil G. Emery

Uncle Bill Nix was six feet and four inches tall and had a big long neck sort of like a crane and a big Adam's apple. He was as straight as a poker when he was standing or on horseback. He was sober most of the time, but when he drank it was always straight whiskey.

Uncle Bill was 76 years old when I first knew him. He had a large burned scar on his left leg above the knee about six inches long that went half way around the top of his leg. It was deep and at least three to four inches of the bone was exposed with no meat or skin over it at all.

Bill had been at a still close to McCamey, Texas to try out the whiskey with three or four more men. They were all drunk. A big pack rat's nest was burning, so when Bill got down and rolled off down the hill, he rolled right into the fire. No one was sober enough to pull him out. He just put some salty meat grease out of the cook pots on a piece of cloth and wrapped it around his leg and fastened it with a couple of big safety pins. If he lost the pins he would just tie knots to keep it on. He could not double his left leg up to pull his boot off so he had to have a boot jack or someone to pull it off. If there was a wagon around, he would use the spokes on the hub of the wheel for a boot jack.

We were working a good-sized herd of stock horses, and Bill wanted a job so he could go to New Mexico with the herd. He asked to take a horse that was branded 2 x 4, a dun horse with black stripes around its legs and down his back and off both shoulder blades. The horse would paw a man and kick him and bite him no matter what you were doing with him. So Bill did not ride him; I wound up with him. Bill was put to taking care of the remuda and he did a good job of it. It is a lot harder to take care of a remuda with a horse herd than with a cattle herd.

I rode up to where Bill was talking to some people stopped on a highway close to Pecos, Texas taking some herd pictures. Bill was telling them that some outlaws caught him and burned him and tortured him trying to make him tell them some secret, but he never gave in.

We went to El Paso to the soap factory with the herd. When we got to the foot of the Guadalupe Mountains, we made camp early enough to shoe some stock and I caught a raw bronc to start on which we had to do every few days to keep a horse back.

An old Mexican fellow came up to my Uncle Monty Bussey (the boss) and bantered him for a trade. He had a nice 5 year old horse that he said was "Muy Bronco." All that was the matter was the saddle that he had ridden the horse with had teeth in it... actually, four single nails that gouged the horse's ribs and left sores in four evenly spaced holes. As soon as he got well, he never offered to buck without a sore back. The old fellow traded for the dun horse that Bill Nix had told my uncle that he owned.

About one hour after he left with the dun horse, a sheriff from Texas with a lawman from New Mexico came looking for a dun stripe-legged horse branded 2 x 4. They looked all through the horses but, of course, he was not there as of one hour earlier.

After the law had left, Monty saw Bill. He said "Bill, you told me that the 2 x 4 horse was yours."

Bill said, "Well, no one was claiming him or had claimed the horse for two or three years. He looked like a pretty good horse so I figured I'd just as well have him as anyone else."

Monty told Bill that he could have gotten us into a lot of trouble if the horse had still been in the bunch. We were real lucky since we had four or five more that were not branded and we brought all of them to the Gila before we branded them out.

When we left El Paso at the Soap factory, Monty Bussey and Uncle Bill Nix left us and came on to the Gila and Julian Bassett sent Bill Nix to the Lyons' Hunting Lodge to look after the property. He stayed there till his death at 79 years of age. I believe that was in 1934. He had been dead for a few days when he was found and was buried close by the lodge.

RAMBLINGS OF A ROLAND STONE

Don't refuse to re-use refuse; recycling has finally arrived in Silver City.

The first black cat of Halloween arrived at Trail End Ranch last week. I heard the tortured, screeching catcalls, went outside to investigate, and saw the silhouette of a big, black cat perched on the topmost spire of a dead ponderosa. Of course, I was mystified; I wondered why a cat would be howling at the new moon from a treetop while turning its pointy-eared head from side to side. Finally, I wised up and realized that the creature wasn't a sitting cat with its tail curled around its ankles; it was a great horned owl who just happened to resemble a black cat. So much for my midnight imagination.

I didn't get much sleep that night, thanks to the house mouse families who were busy holding a reunion and a bowling tournament.

There are two main mouse families residing in our happy home: the kitchen stove mice and the den stove mice. Even though they intermingle and intermarry, there seems to be a friendly rivalry between the two clans to see which can produce the loudest cacophony by banging on the sheet metal of the other sides' stove all night long. Naturally, I've thought about turning on the gas on the stove to fight fur with fire.

After tiring of filling boots, nooks, and all empty places throughout the house with Wyndi's purloined chow, the mice have invented a new activity to play with Wyndi's Purina biscuit balls. The aim of their new game is for the two teams to bowl bickies (biscuits) from one gas stove across the wood floors to the other heater. Points are scored when a missile makes a direct hit and produces a satisfying clarion gong bong sound from the thin tin.

Sometimes during the night the sound of innocuous activity changed and assumed the deafening fury of a hailstorm. I leaped out of bed, dashed into the den and into the midst of The Great Purina War. It seems the spectators had gotten bored and had bored into Wyndi's fresh, hundred pound sack of bickies which must have looked to them like a giant Trojan horse full of ammunition. Wyndi lost her patience after losing her food, but rushing after the mice was like rolling on marbles as the mice scattered and scurried into their steel stove strongholds.

After an hour with a push broom and snow shovel, our happy home is again immaculate.

The next night I baited the box trap with a handful of sunflower seeds. It worked -- I caught and evicted eight mice. They feel right at home in the comfortable old box. One veteran mouse even had the audacity to carry in his fluffy bedroll and set up camp in the cozy trap. I had to wake him up and shake him out at the feed and fun area.

Now that winter is peeking around the corner, the mice want to move inside the buildings at Trail End Ranch. They won't listen to me, and chew up my eviction notices, so next time I go to town I'll borrow a cat.

What's the difference between a cat and a little kitten? A cat'll scratch, but a little kitten'll never hurt anyone.

CECIL EMERY TALKS...

A LITTLE ABOUT THE GILA WILDERNESS

Although I have lived, worked, and fished in the Gila Wilderness for many years, I've never quit being interested in the country. It has some of the most beautiful places that anyone can imagine; when you're working it, though, it is some of the hardest work that you can imagine. It's hard on men and animals. The best you can do is pack in grain to feed your stock. You have to depend on the forage there for the livestock.

In some places, there is good grass; but, in many places, all you can find is pine grass that has turpentine in it. A horse or mule will eat pine grass, but his teeth will get sore. Unless you soak the hard grain some, they cannot eat right, and they will not do well when you are using them hard. I will guarantee you that that is the only way you can use saddle and pack animals since you are either going up or down grade wherever you go. The best of trails are not very smooth. Lots of our work was done on lesser trails, especially when we were going to fires.

I stayed on Mogollon Baldy for two fires seasons. I was lookout both years, but did swap off with fire chasers when their horses were tired and they were, too. I would also pack water and take the stock to water at springs.

After lookout hours, I stayed with Theron Stockbridge in 1931 and with Curley (Lawrence) Bryant in 1934. We started fire seasons in April of 1934. There was very little snow that year so we were put in a camp building gateless areas and staying on fire call.

Gateless areas were fences built around areas to prevent these plots from being used for grazing but it did not keep wildife out. It just made a place that had to be gone around; so it kept some stock out, but it was a lot of expense with no gain.

I built some fence and then the cook quit so I went to cooking. After packing for a while, I got a couple of days off in May and I went down to Cliff and Ruth Watson and I got married on the 12th. But on the 12th a fire broke out and Henry Woodrow was looking for me. Ruth's father (John Watson) got a hold of me on the 13th so I left for a camp on the east prong of Mogollon Creek.

The fire there was under control so I was told to move to Mogollon Baldy for lookout duty. Curley Bryant also went to Baldy as a fire chaser, until he got word that his wife was about to have their first child over in Buckhorn. I took over as lookout until Curley came back three days later and then there we were. It was 90 days before he got back to see his new boy and 95 days before I got to see my new wife!

I could see my house with high-powered binoculars 40 miles due south of Baldy. There is a geodetic survey mark at Baldy and one just above the schoolhouse at Cliff that was established in 1934. My wife was living in a house at the mouth of Duck Creek where it emptied into the Gila River. Every once in a while I'd spot smoke near Cliff and one day I spotted smoke just above Cliff on the Gila River. When I called in the reading, he answered right back that he would see about sending someone to see about it. "I don't suppose you would like to go," he asked. He was just joking for it was only a haystack fire at the rice farm.

It was real dry all year in 1934 so there were lots of fires. Some were small and some were very large; a few were manmade. Most of the men walked in but a few rode horses in. All the chuck and tools to fight the fires had to be packed in. The fire camps were not very elaborate. Fresh meat had to be killed in the mountains. They killed some Heart Bar Cross or 916 ranch beef and made government vouchers out to whoever's beef it was.

There were 110 head of pack burros there and most of them were used continually for about four months as fire season was not over until late August. There had to be two men with each pack string because the bear were out everywhere. The bear would dig for grubs and roll logs, and if the pack animals saw them or heard a strange noise they would try to turn back. If no one was in the lead to scare the bear off, you sure would have a wreck as the trails were pretty narrow in a lot of places.

We had camps on Little Creek and Mogollon Creeks in different places and on Iron Creek and Willow Creek we built gateless areas and fish dams. Some of the fish dams that were put in that year are still intact.

When I got to go out for a couple of days in the first part of August, I had had a 95 day honeymoon by myself, so of course I caught a lot of ribbing. When I came back to camp, I got orders to bring my bed and come to White Creek to cook and do whatever came up which amounted to packing and chasing fires.

I worked with some awfully good packers -- a lot of good men. One of the packers that I remember was Frank Hooker. Another was Lloyd Hunter. Lloyd was 6'4" and always packed from one side only. He carried a flat iron and washed and ironed his pants and shirt on a pack box and pack cover. Bill Furr, Lee Gatlin, and Buck Maxwell packed some, but they mostly stayed in camp where Frank Moore was cooking on Iron Creek and Willow Creek. I went to Frank's camp and he had bluejays and squirrels lighting on his shoulders and riding around camp till a stranger showed up, then they would hide out.

There were several more men in camp -- Doc Cooper and Wesley Fleming, for instance. Another was George Clark who was in charge of one camp and crew. George had a haircutting kit in his bed. When we got in a bad place, his bed mule rolled off the trail on a switchback and George said, "There go my hair clippers!" Sure enough, that night we found out his clippers had two teeth broken out. Those clippers sure would pull hair out after that! We all suffered since that was our barber shop for a while; no one wore braids in those days.

Cont'd →

→ Cont'd

One day Lee Gatlin needed to go up to White Creek which is right up under Mogollon Baldy to get some horses. Henry Woodrow had a horse that was sort of fresh and as Lee's horse was jaded, Henry told Lee to ride the horse to harden him up and take the edge off him. Lee jumped a bear up at the head of the canyon where the shin oaks and boulders were knee to belly deep. The horse was sort of skinned up so Henry was sort of upset. He told me he didn't think he would loan Lee a horse anymore.

We had a dude ranch down on the main Mogollon Creek and they had a sub camp on White Creek above the White Creek ranger station. The girls and women did not dress very heavily; in fact, they rode in bikinis. How they could stand it, I don't know. They would come up to Baldy in a halter, a G string, and shoes -- and it was always cold up there. At the camp they had a swimming hole and they all just skinny-dipped.

Where White Creek comes into the west fork of the Gila was the Jenks cabin. That was where the the fish hatchery was located for many years. The spring there was just one degree off from freezing the year round. In the wintertime, steam rises from it; the snow stacks up around it and the springs are still just above freezing. In the fall, the fish hatchery would buy the horses they needed to feed the fish for the winter. It was a market for old renegade horses. As long as they were healthy and carrying good flesh they bought them. When the snow began to fly, they butchered all of them and hung them up to grind for the little fishes.

Ed Ault was over at the hatchery for several years; he always had someone to help in the winter. He had Curley Bryant there for some winters. Ed had a family above Cliff on the Gila so he would walk in and out with snowshoes. Sometimes he would go around by Baldy and Snow Park just to check on the snow depth or sometimes just because he liked to go there. Ed was a real good artist. He drew pictures of butterflies and animals or whatever he thought of with a sharp stick on the aspen trees. He always carved the date when the art was done. These pictures would raise up on the bark and some of them would be 20 to 30 feet up on the trees in the summertime. I asked him how he reached that high. That was easy, he said -- He just stood on the top of the snow.

The fish hatchery had three big pack mules that would weigh between 1300 and 1400 pounds and pack up to 500 pound loads from the 916 ranch. Once they were packing new corrugated tin in ten foot lengths to put a roof on a building at the hatchery. It was working on the mules' ears so Ed said he asked Barker if he could cut the sheets in two and that way not cut up the mules' ears. He said Barker told him the mules' ears would grow back on.

One time Curley Bryant was packing fish out to plant in Mogollon Creek when one of the mules slipped and fell off the trail on a bluff. He finally landed several feet below on his back. When Curley got down where he was, he had gotten up and was not too bad off. All the fish cans were busted as well as the pack saddle. A few of the fish died, but most of them got in the water and swam off. The mule was able to go back to work in a few days.

There sure was good fishing in the streams of the Gila Wilderness as long as the hatchery was at Jenks cabin. There was lots of game in the mountains then, too. There weren't any elk then, but everything else was plentiful. My Uncle Monty Bussey and I counted 140 deer within one mile at one time on Prior Mesa not far from Prior Cabin.

Prior Cabin was home to George Clark and Bud "Reasonable" Reason (nearly everyone knew him by "Reasonable Bud"), an Ohio cowboy who worked for Julian Basset when he had the Heart Bar Cross, the Moon Ranch, and the Gila farms here in Grant County. They built a double log cabin with a double fireplace there. One part was always open with some chuck in it, but one part was locked.

On one trip, Frank Hooker and I packed from Turkey Creek and Hidden Pasture and then came up through Deadman Canyon. We had about 30 packs and Frank was in the lead when we met two old maverick bulls on the 916 range who were always on the prod. Frank finally drove them off without us having a wreck.

Cont'd →

PHELPS DODGE PROSECUTES
HOT SPRINGS TRESPASSERS
by Arvella Zachari and Steve Garner

We were basking in the short-lived winter sun, bathing in the Hot Springs of Faywood, feeling grateful for this gentle, healing break in a busy, productive, albeit hectic, day to day life. We felt grateful for the chance to reconnect with the healing strength of the hot springs, gifts given naturally for the purpose of nurturing and encouraging the people.

I remember hearing of the Toltecs who also saw the beneficial qualities of a Hot Spring placed there for rest, peace and healing in the midst of desert mountains beneath a vast, starlit sky. How could any of us see it to be anything but a gift? Think of how many people have roamed these lands knowing and enjoying this gift? How many people who were born here or who bore their children here consider the hot springs an all-important tie with the land -- a source of rejuvenation and regeneration that promotes a healthy society?

These were some of my thoughts as I dressed and began walking in the direction of the car. Suddenly, I was approached by the Grant County Sheriff's Department. I didn't feel like a criminal since all I had done was give my children a much needed hot bath.

The sheriff was very polite and considerate. He called Phelps Dodge to ask them if he could just let it slide with a warning. He was given a quick reponse of, "Why aren't you people upholding the law?" When the security guard got there, he told the sheriff to prosecute us by giving my friends and I a $30 citation for criminal trespassing.

The sheriff didn't seem to mind that we had been bathing there nor did the judge he so kindly called for an opinion. They just had to uphold the law.

The law states that the hot spring is on Phelps Dodge land and they want it posted. One may ask why they are not willing to share. Perhaps they have need of it for themselves or maybe they're afraid of being sued for something harmful coming to the people who bathe there.

The free use of hot springs in the entire Gila River Basin is under a most immediate threat. Hot springs are a rich part of our Southwestern heritage. We cannot afford to be posted, ruled, and regulated out of a God-given right to take a hot bath.

Perhaps the state should consider providing a caretaker for the hot springs. I know many who would consider it an honor to caretake a hot spring. Perhaps a nominal fee coud be required of bathers or a donation -- some way of not drawing commercial capitalistic gain out of a Nature-given, sacred resource. The state needs to maintain at least some portion of this land for us, all of us, to experience the healing waters offered by Mother Earth.

GIVE FAYWOOD HOT SPRINGS
BACK TO THE PEOPLE!

61

A few days later I was with Bill Furr on the same trail. I heard a lot of noise up ahead, when here comes Bill Furr. The bulls had wrecked our pack outfit! One bull was combing the hair out of the old horse's tail. They finally left, but it took us quite a while to get our outfit on its feet and going on up the trail. Bill told Henry Woodrow that we ought to kill the bulls but Henry said we would never get through paying if we did that. We would just have to put up with them the best we could.

This trail went to Little Creek fire cabin and on down to either the Gila River or to Granite Peak lookout which forked out to White Creek. Fred Chappel stayed at Little Creek fire cabin for the fire seaon of '34 and he told me he did not intend to do that anymore.

Theron Stockbridge was also in a camp there in 1934 for a while. He was the first forest ranger at White Creek of record. He finally quit and went to prospecting. When I knew him, he had a cabin on Sacaton Canyon where he lived and prospected. I only remember three of his children -- Theron, Howard, and Catherine who married Dave Steward of Bald Knoll country who was half brother to Bob Wallace. (I saw some of Dave and Catherine's children at Safford a few years ago.)

The telephone lines in the mountains were strung on trees so when you had to work on them you would start up with a belt and climbing spurs. Sometimes when the line was attached 10 and 15 feet high in a tree, you could climb the hill and reach out and touch the tree... but when you climbed onto it and looked down it might be a 30 --100 feet drop if you fell out. These trees were not trimmed so you would have to jump your belt to get it over the knots and snags.

One day Curley Bryant was working on a tree down the mountain but in sight of me up in the tower. I saw him start down after he had fixed an insulator but then his spurs did not hold and he came down real fast till his belt hung on a snag and he stopped real suddenly. He could not get his spur to hold so he was there when I got out of the tower and went down to help him. He sure was skinned up where the bark and snags had gotten his face and chin; his belly was skinned, too. When I got his spur to hold, he climbed up enough to get the belt over the snag. He said he was glad I had been able to see him, otherwise he would just have to have stayed there. He was about three feet from the ground on the upper side of the tree.

Lightning sure gets to playing around on the points and ridges, especially if there are rock spines and trees right at the backbone of a ridge. Sometimes the lightning would melt the wire off the trees. Once at Mogollon Baldy it melted a metal phone and the metal ran down the log wall in the cabin; it tore out the phone up in the tower.

Lightning also knocked off Edwin Shelly's boot sole when he was in the tower. There was a large hole in the side of the building on top of the tower and all the nails in the roof were melted. Edwin told me that when he came to and saw the hole in the house, he opened the tarp door and made it down to the ground and ran to the cabin. When he hit the jagged rocks, he looked down and saw he had the tops of his boots up around his shins and no soles left! There was about a quarter of a mile of phone wire burnt up, too. The cabin and tower were both grounded with large copper rods that were twisted together at the apex of the roofs and run off at each corner. They extended away for several feet to conduct the lightning away from the buildings. The tower house was patched for a long time with some old packing boxes and tar paper. We had a dugout in the side of the hill close by the cabin and we would go in it sometimes for safety.

I saw a freshly unsaddled horse get hit by lightning that bounced off the cabin and knocked the horse down. A little bit later the horse got up an staggered off. The hair was burned off on both sides of the horse's neck. The next morning the horse seemed okay. It belonged to Rollin Hubbard, a trailworker who lived in Gila with a large family.

In 1931 the snow was real deep over the crest just ten feet away from the cabin when the season was over the last of June, but there was no snow there in 1934 even in May. It did hail one or two times that summer, but very little; it would get real cold when it did hail. When there was snow close to the cabin, we used it as our freezer even though just 20 feet away the flies would be swarming.

There were at least two kinds of flies -- one big gray one that would bite an animal and draw blood. There was also a blowfly that

Cont'd →

ON THE DESERT
by David Eppele

TREATY ON CROSS-BORDER AQUIFERS URGED

"U.S. - Mexican border communities are going to face increasingly serious groundwater supplies and contamination problems unless both countries agree to regulate pumping."

This statement comes from Albert E. Utton, law professor at the University of New Mexico in Albuquerque. Utton is also the director of the newly formed U.S. - Mexico Trans-Boundary Resources Center in Albuquerque, New Mexico.

The lack of any bilateral treaty regulating the cross-border aquifers at El Paso, Texas, the Santa Cruz and San Pedro river basins in southern Arizona, and aquifers in California and Texas amounts to "legal anarchy," Utton said. He termed the current groundwater practices all along the U.S. - Mexico border an "out of sight, out of mind" problem that can only get worse as rapid population growth continues in the U.S. Sun Belt.

The situation is aggravated by the border area's almost total reliance on groundwater for various municipal and commercial uses.

Utton pointed out that the population of El Paso is nearly 600,000 and that Juarez, Mexico has an estimated population of over *two million* people.

"Groundwater extraction on one side of the border greatly affects the water table across the border. Corss-border communities share aquifers that are rapidly becoming depleted," he added.

There is a well field being drilled in northern Sonora, Mexico at the source of the San Pedro River which flows north into Arizona. The water from these wells is being used in mining activities at Cananea, Mexico. Utton said this practice could destroy or drastically change downstream riparian areas." One of the prime (and nearly the last) riparian area that could be adversely affected is the recently opened San Pedro Riparian National Conservation Area.

Utton also said the International Boundary and Water Commission in El Paso, Texas has little or no authority to regulate groundwater pumping or recharge of cross-border aquifers and its authority should be expanded.

There are others who say that expanding the authority of the IBWC would not work because that commission would react "politically" and not necessarily in the interest of all parties concerned.

The 1973 agreement to regulate pumping at San Luis Rio Colorado and Yuma on the Colorado River is the only existing bilateral groundwater accord between the United States and Mexico.

I asked Utton what the four states along the U.S. - Mexican border felt about a treaty on cross-border aquifers. And, most importantly, what did Mexico have to say?

"California, Arizona, and New Mexico all seem to be willing to enter into an International Treaty, but Texas is unwilling."

"Why?" I asked.

"Texans don't want to be told how they can use their water resources," replied Utton. Utton said that Mexico is "ready to address this problem."

Now... are we ready?

● ●

➤ Cont'd

would blow eggs into the wounds under a horse's saddle. When you pulled the saddle off a sore, sweaty horse, you would find them blowing eggs onto their backs before the sweat dried. They would even blow eggs onto a wet bedroll.

I wrote a little verse on the side of the dugout wall that I have been told was there several years after I worked at Baldy. It went like this: "I was here in 1931 and I was here in 1934, and I ain't ever going to be here any more." Well, I never did get back, although I would like to have taken my family to see that country for it is beautiful. Snow Park which is just under the top of the mountain is exceptional.   It has grass waist high to a tall man and lots of quaking asps and fir trees.

We used to keep extra horses there in the summertime but not any colts for the mountain lions would kill all of them. Worty Shelly and his brother-in-law, Carl McClain, bought a young horse that was running in Snow Park from Fred Turnbaugh and came up to Baldy to get it while I was staying there in 1934. They did not have a pack horse so they did not bring bedding but they did have the first air mattress that I had ever seen. I had only heard of them till then. No one got much sleep that night as they were up and down all night pumping that thing up. They got the horse the next day and went back to the 916 ranch. I used some air mattresses in later years and they were all right if you never put them down close to sand burs or grass burs.

My youngest son, Gary, worked for the Forest Service several years after my time. He was at Willow Creek, Bear Wallow, Negrito, and Bursom Road country. He had a pickup so he hauled supplies and chased fires and did lookout duty. My pay was about $70 / month plus chuck and horse grain if I used my horse which was customary. Gary's pay was more but he had a lot more expenses even if he did not break down. I was young and strong then and I did enjoy the time. Since then I put in quite a lot of time fishing and camping in the Gila Wilderness and wore out a few horses and mules going in and out. I did a lot of walking, too.

I also put in some time on the Black Range when that country was wilderness. The G.O.S. Cattle Company took in some of it for a lot of years till it was divided up and sold to other interests. At the top of the Black Range there were division fences and on the east side was the Ladder Ranch. At the head of the Mimbres on the north side of Reeds Peak was Diamond Bar Range. We hardly ever worked on the

adjoining ranges except as reps for the ranches we worked for. I've been over some of the country but I never worked much north of the division fence or the Diamond Bar and the G.O.S. which went across Rocky Canyon and the mouth of Black Canyon to the east fork of the Gila close to the old Lyons hunting lodge. There it jogged around to the west side of the Gila River close to Sycamore Canyon and then out around and above the Granny benches and back into the Gila near Water Canyon. All these ranches have been broken up and a lot of different owners have had parts of this ranch for several years now.

The fish dams were a little more sensible and helped to make deeper holes to protect the fish from coons and fish hawks and fish ducks.   The deeper water made it possible for the fish to survive in low water times; being deeper holes, the water was kept cooler in warm weather. Willow Creek in Catron County still has some of the original dams that were built in 1934. Little Creek has some yet that were put in the same year. Of course, a few have washed out and some of the logs were broken in flood time.

There were many other good men who worked for the Forest Service in the Gila Wilderness in 1931 and 1934 -- two, at least, and maybe several more I have forgotten. Nat Straw was an old-timer in 1934. He worked for the Forest Service in several states as well as for big ranches as a wildlife live trapper mostly, but sometimes he trapped livestock killers on the ranches, like bear and lion. When I was there, he worked for the Forest Service catching beaver and transplanting them to different locations in New Mexico and other states also. He was a very interesting man to talk to as he had been in a lot of western states. Sometimes he and Ranger Henry Woodrow would get into old time talks which was very interesting to me.

Another man who packed for the Forest Service in 1931 was Red (Tom) Ross. He had a little ranch in Grant County close to the Gila River and Blue Creek. He was between the two so he broke horses and pack mules both for himself and other people, too. He had a bunch of bronc mules leased to the Forest Service and for breaking them all at the same time he got 50 cents a day plus grain and wages. The mules were broken by the time the season was over. But the season was not very long that year. I wound up working at the H--Y ranch on Blue Creek that fall and Red was working there, too, furnishing his pack saddles. The outfit had one old McClellan Army saddle rigged up for a pack saddle and they had a pack outfit when we were working cattle. There were no roads at that time on that ranch .

Art by Susan Eigenbrodt from *The Wilderness Outlook*, July 10–24, 1989.